Short-Term Losses

Short-Term Losses

Stories

Mark Lindensmith

Southern Methodist
University Press

Dallas

These stories are works of fiction. Names, characters, places, and incidents are either the product of the author's imagination or are used fictitiously.

Copyright © 1996 by Mark Lindensmith
All rights reserved
First edition, 1996

Requests for permission to reproduce material from this work should be sent to:
    Rights and Permissions
    Southern Methodist University Press
    PO Box 750415
    Dallas, TX 75275-0415

Some of the stories in this collection first appeared in the following publications: "One Small Step," "Short-Term Losses," and "Singleton" in *South Dakota Review* (Spring 1990, Winter 1990, and Summer 1993, respectively; reprinted with permission); "On King Hill" (as "What the Thunder Said") in *New Letters* (Summer 1990; reprinted with the permission of *New Letters* and the Curators of the University of Missouri–Kansas City); "The Casaloma" in *Wind* (1991; reprinted with permission); and "Gathering Bittersweet" in *Thema* (Fall 1994; reprinted with permission).

Library of Congress Cataloging-in-Publication Data

Lindensmith, Mark, 1953–
    Short-term losses : stories / Mark Lindensmith. — 1st ed.
      p. cm.
    ISBN 0-87074-406-2 (cloth : alk. paper). —
ISBN 0-87074-407-0 (pbk. : alk. paper)
      1. Manners and customs—Fiction. I. Title.
PS3562.I51114S56   1996
813'.54—dc20   96-15669

Cover illustration and design by Barbara Whitehead

Printed in the United States of America on acid-free paper
10 9 8 7 6 5 4 3 2 1

For Dad and Phil

*The things I am most
proud of in this life,
I have done with Gaytha.
Making this book is one
of those things.*

Acknowledgments

*Thanks to the
Virginia Center for the Creative Arts
for the time and space to create, and
thanks to Mark Dewey, Les Whipp, and
John Gilgun for encouraging me
to keep at it.*

Contents

One Small Step   1

Short-Term Losses   17

Failing to Close   33

Singleton   57

On King Hill   77

The Casaloma   93

Windows   107

Dead Coach   129

Transmigration   145

Gathering Bittersweet   171

One Small Step

IT WAS a startling summer, and things seemed to change at our house after the moon flight. That was the summer my mother told me I was conceived in the same hospital where I was born. She said it happened like this. She was in the hospital having her tonsils taken out, and my father, fresh back from Norfolk, Virginia, in his crisp crew cut and navy whites, took her into his arms on a blanket on the floor of her room, his foot jammed against the inside of the door for privacy. She was still slightly tipsy with a fever, they hadn't seen each other in months, and my mother's roommate had checked out earlier in the day. So none of it could be helped really, she said. But they had been married for almost a year and were already old enough to vote. She wanted to emphasize that, because she told me all of this the summer I was fourteen, and she wanted to make sure I was clear on certain things.

That summer, my mother began to leave little paperback books lying around the house—the kind that were explicit, very detailed. She would leave copies of *Psychology Today* that had cover stories on human sexuality on top of the stack of magazines in the TV room. That was the summer the Eagle landed at Tranquility Base and there was one small step for man. It was the summer Ted Kennedy drove off into black water with a blonde friend. And for me, it was the summer I got an erection every time I thought of our lovely neighbor, Consuela Matthews.

I remember my father's hands, too, and how they started to change a little that summer, especially after the flight and the landing. I already knew my father's hands by heart, of course. Children always do. That's one thing a father should know if he ever plays Santa Claus or tries to dress up to fool his kids. Wear gloves. Children know a father's hands better than they know anything else about him—better than his eyes, or nose, or even his voice. And that summer I remember really watching and admiring my father's hands.

His hands were in great demand. They could spin my mother around and draw her to him and make her laugh, and they could grip a hammer and drive nails straight and true in five steady whacks. His hands were brown and hard and large enough that power tools fit there nicely, as if in a clamp. They weren't overly large, though, and there was nothing awkward about them. They just looked like they belonged there, attached to his knobbed wrists and firm forearms, the hand and arm all tied together with pencil-thick veins that wrapped around his wrists. His thumbs curled out, like rockers on a chair, as if they were made to play a sweet, curling brass instrument. He had the hands of a sportsman.

Instead of hunting and fishing, though, my father liked to fix things. He was a supervisor for the three-to-eleven shift at the Westab plant there in St. Joseph, Missouri, a place where they made huge rolls of milled paper into smaller packets of paper, like note pads or Big Chief tablets. So while most of the other fathers were off at their jobs during the day, my father used the daylight hours to fix and paint and shine things.

The other thing he liked to do—and this was something that fascinated the other kids in the neighborhood—was he liked to play the drums. He had a full set of pearl white Slingerland drums (Zildjian cymbals, double tom-toms, and all) set up in our basement, and he taught me to play when I was just a little boy. He had been in a jazz band for a while before he went into the navy, but then I was born. Sometimes on a cool, bright summer morning—the kind of morning when all the windows were thrown open and it felt good just to walk along the clean sidewalk under the huge maples out front—our house would vibrate with the heavy, steady beat of the bass and the snappy little explosions of flams and paradiddles, rolls and rim shots. His hands were fast, his wrists were spring-loaded. My mother complained about the noise, but I could tell she really liked it. She would be in the kitchen putting away clean dishes, or in the back room folding and stacking laundry, and you could see her start moving to his beat. Sometimes he played along with old Benny Goodman records turned up as loud as they would go on the stereo set downstairs. He could almost keep up with Gene Krupa on "Sing, Sing, Sing."

And in their quieter moments, while my mother wrote checks or while my father worked on something small with lots of tiny screws, they listened to Dave Brubeck or the Modern Jazz Quartet, maybe a little Ella Fitzgerald. My parents could take five better than anyone I knew, just sitting for long stretches, happy to say nothing, while Paul Desmond blew high, cool sax all over our house in that defiant 5/4 time. They touched each other naturally, without thought, as they carried out little tasks from room to room.

My father and mother, Tony and Anne, were a handsome couple and looked younger than their thirty-seven years. They read books, and by the time I was fourteen, they told me a few things. For instance, besides telling me I was conceived on the floor of the Methodist hospital, my mother once told me that when my baby brother died, only two days after being born, her minister came into her hospital room to console her, took her in his arms, and confessed his love for her. He was an older man with wavy hair and a teenage daughter and had been our preacher for years. He told her that he would leave his wife for her, but my mother told him that she thought he was just overcome by emotion. She would never mention it again if he didn't. I have no idea why my mother told me such things, except perhaps just to let me know that unexpected and confusing things happened sometimes.

My father told me things, too. He encouraged me to hand him his tools as he worked, and once, when we were changing the spark plugs in an old DeSoto he used as a second car, he told me why people always had to scrape their knuckles when they worked on cars.

"It's a spiritual thing," he said. "Old cars demand a blood sacrifice before they'll work right." And sure enough, before it was over, his socket wrench slipped, and he took a white gash out of the top of his middle knuckle. The cut turned pink, then red, then dripped three wine drops onto the hot manifold pipes. When it happened, Dad sucked in air through clenched teeth and said, "Son of a bitch!" That was his standard response to such injuries. Then he wiped his hand on a dirty rag and said, "You watch. This old thing will run tight as a tick now." And he was right, but, of course, it had new spark plugs.

And another time, and this was that same summer I'm thinking about now, I met him in the kitchen while he was eating vanilla ice cream straight out of the carton. It was midmorning, and the sun was getting bright and hot. He had on his usual outfit—white T-shirt and button-up Levi's—and his brown hair, which was starting to get long, was feathered back over his ears slightly. Dad just stood at the kitchen window, staring out across the Matthewses' backyard and taking one slow spoonful of ice cream after another to his mouth. I looked out to see what he was staring at, but there was nothing there except the Matthewses' empty patio and a lawn full of brightly colored plastic toys that belonged to Bobby, the Matthewses' little boy. Dad wouldn't have been eating straight out of the carton if Mom was home, but she was down at Wrinkle's Drugstore, where she did the bookkeeping for old Mrs. Wrinkle two mornings a week.

After a few more slow-motion spoons of ice cream, he turned to me and said, "Here's a life poem for you. Why do I do this so slowly? Because the end comes so quickly." He took one more bite of ice cream and seemed to think about it for a second. "I just made it up," he said. "Has sort of a Zen flavor to it."

"The ice cream?"

"No, the poem. What do you think?"

"I think it's short and doesn't rhyme," I said.

"Good point," he said, "but it's true about a lot of things." He held the open carton of ice cream toward me. "Want some?"

"No thanks," I said, and left him there with his thoughts and his melting ice cream. I didn't tell him what I really wanted at that moment. What I really wanted was for Consuela Matthews to come out onto her patio to sunbathe in her shockingly white and brief bikini while I sat quietly and discreetly at the edge of my upstairs window, which faced the Matthewses' patio.

Ours was a neighborhood of neat, white two-story clapboard houses, some with green shingles and some with slate-colored shingles, heavily landscaped with shapely old hardwood trees along the boundaries and tight springy evergreen shrubs around the foundations. Only a few houses along our block had window air-conditioners at that time, but most of the houses had patios, and my father had helped to install many of them. The decade seemed to have been one for building patios and for having patio parties. Elsewhere in the world there were assassinations, and riots, and protests, but where we lived, there were patio parties. They were the kind of parties that started before dark, with iced Pearl beer in huge tubs and steaks on the white brick built-in barbecue, and ended after midnight, with the last flicker from colorful little Japanese lanterns.

This was all during a time when almost all the adults smoked, and the women of the neighborhood sunbathed, working up vicious tans to go with their pale gloss lipstick and pearly white nail polish. And so, during this time of fenceless backyards, and patios, and bathing in the sun, I was lucky enough to live next door to Consuela Matthews, the youngest and sexiest mother on the block. Everyone called her Connie.

Robert and Connie Matthews and their little boy, Bobby, who must have been about three years old that summer that men first walked on the moon, came to our block two years earlier from Houston, Texas, and brought with them tequila, a wicked recipe for chili, and a collection of the skimpiest bikini bathing suits south St. Joseph had ever seen. Robert taught philosophy and humanities at the state college on the outskirts of town, and Connie helped to make ends meet by giving piano and flute lessons at Prindle's Music Store downtown. Still, they never seemed to have quite enough money to keep the house up like most of the other houses on the block—or to get a new car. They drove a beat-up old black Renault, and they just had the one car, so Robert would carpool sometimes with one of the secretaries who worked at the college.

Robert and Connie usually came to the neighborhood parties, but sometimes they had parties of their own. They had small parties that would light up their house, upstairs and down. Men with wire-rim glasses and sculpted beards, like Robert's, and women with long hair, feathers, and fringed leather arrived at the Matthewses' parties. They all drove beat-up old foreign cars. They played classical music and Beatles albums and talked and talked. I could lie in my bed with the window open during warm evenings and hear all the talking from the Matthewses' parties. I couldn't hear what they said, but I could hear the steady hum of men and women talking all at once, their volume rising and falling with the volume and intensity of the music. And sometimes, after the guests were gone, I could still hear Robert and Connie, their words indistinct, but their tone that of anger and accusation. Their voices rose in pitch to a climactic level of frustration, then dropped off in silence with a slam of a door and switch of a light.

The next day, there she would be, on her cot in the blistering midday sun, her long black hair shiny on top as if she were crowned with a halo; and there I would be, at my window, just waiting for each little turn, each tiny flex of muscle. She had a swimmer's body, with slightly broad shoulders and narrow hips, and a stomach so flat that when she lay on her back the tiny strip of cloth across her pelvis formed a kind of taut bridge between her two jutting hip bones. Her suits were so brief it wasn't unusual at all to catch a glimpse of brown nipple or strands of wiry black hair peeking from beneath colorful lycra triangles. Sometimes, when she moved from her back to her front on the plastic cot, an entire creamy scoop of breast would jump loose momentarily, and she would adjust herself with a slight shift of cloth and a flick of elastic.

So that's what I was doing on the morning the astronauts were on their way back from the moon. I was watching Connie Matthews while she was tanning, and my mother was making lunch down in the kitchen. Mom had her bathing suit on, too, just itching to get back out into the sun. Her suit was more modest than Connie's, but she still looked fetching in it. Her body was firm, her sun-bleached hair was puffed out in back and flipped under at the ends. Mom had the radio turned on to keep track of the Apollo capsule's progress toward earth, and I could just picture her moving from counter to counter in that brisk way she had about her, one ear cocked toward the crackling conversation between Houston and space, her bare feet padding across the tile. Connie, on the other hand, didn't move a muscle. It was as if the heat had paralyzed her, with her face toward the sun, her sunglasses in place, her hands cupped at her thighs. A pool of perspiration welled in her brown, brown navel.

There were other things going on, too. Almost straight across from my window, I could see little Bobby Matthews playing in his room. Once in a while, he would pass in front of his screened window jabbering to himself or to an imaginary friend. And somewhere on the other side of our house, my father was spraying the foundation to get rid of some black ants that had begun to invade our basement. He had a pump sprayer with a tank of chlordane slung across his shoulder. This was before chlordane was taken off the market—before any of us really knew how dangerous sunbathing and spraying for ants could be.

Although I was focused on Connie, I saw Bobby

Matthews out of the corner of my eye. He had come to his window and was looking straight at me. I must have looked like a disembodied head just resting there on the window casement. Then he was up in his window on his knees, and he was trying to say something to me through the screen. He put his hands up, as if to reach for something, and tried to pull himself to a standing position on the casement. I remember looking directly at him, assessing his position, quickly calculating his three-year-old weight, and thinking: I should say something.

Before I could yell or move, though, I heard the zip of the ripping screen, and Bobby Matthews took one small step, somersaulting out of his second-floor window without a sound. I found my voice as he descended, and yelled "Watch out!" I don't know what good I thought yelling would do at that point, but it got Connie's attention. She turned quickly, leaning on one elbow, and looked in my direction just as Bobby landed on his back on the evergreen shrub below his window. It was an old shrub, the kind that gets cluttered with bagworms, and it hadn't been pruned for some time. Bobby hit with an "umph!" and disappeared into the bush. There was a pause, a moment's delay, and then Bobby cut loose with a scream that brought Connie up off her cot and sent me thumping down our stairs three at a time.

"Bobby fell out of his window!" I yelled at my mother as I ran out the back door. She was wiping her hands on a paper towel.

By the time I got to the side yard, Connie had already plucked Bobby from the bushes and sat in the grass rocking him back and forth, his head clutched to her bosom. The boy was rigid and red with screaming, and perspiration dripped from Connie's lip onto his dark hair. Her sunglasses were knocked askew, and as I ran up to her there on the grass, she looked at me as if I was supposed to start answering questions.

"He fell out the window," I said. "I saw him."

"Where's your Dad?" she said in a breathy rush. "Where's Tony?"

I was breathing hard, and I motioned with my hand toward the back of the house. By then my mother was running toward us, still carrying the crumpled, wet paper towel.

Connie Matthews just sat in the grass, rocking the child back and forth, and began to yell for my father. She looked at my mother pleadingly and said again, "Where's Tony?"

It was only later that it struck me as odd that she would call out for my father. Usually women will turn to other women for aid in such emergencies, knowing that fathers tend to panic more readily than mothers at the sight of a child's blood. At that moment, though, I thought I understood why she called out for Dad—it was because he was handy, he was available, he could fix things. He had the tools to take care of what was broken.

Just then he came trotting around the corner of the house, his tank of chlordane bouncing off his shoulder, the sprayer nozzle held aloft like an Olympian's torch. He dropped the equipment and walked toward us saying, "All right, calm down. Calm down." He looked at each of us clustered there between the houses, trying to sum up at a glance what had happened.

"Bobby jumped out the window!" Connie said, sobbing now at the sight of my father and holding the child even more tightly against her.

"He didn't jump," I told my father. "He was just playing in the window, and he fell through the screen. I saw it happen."

Dad's eyes registered an understanding. He knew exactly what I was talking about. He looked up at the torn screen, then down at the partially flattened shrub.

"Did he land in there?" Dad said. I told him yes, and Dad crouched down in front of the mother and child, elbows on his knees. Mom was on her knees in the grass gently lifting the lopsided sunglasses from Connie's face and murmuring that everything was going to be OK. Bobby's screams had already started to diminish.

Dad touched Connie's forearm lightly and said, "Don't squeeze so hard. You might hurt him." He moved in a little closer to Bobby, whose crying was beginning to subside into tearful, jerking gasps for air, and said, "Hey partner, can you move your hands and feet for me a little? Don't move your head. Just wiggle your hands and feet a little." The boy did as he was asked, my father's attention already distracting him from the fall. "Can you tell me where it hurts?" Dad said.

"Scratches," Bobby said, shuddering as if chilled.

"You mean these scratches on your arms and legs?" Dad said, pointing to the red and pink cuts that had been etched into the boy's arm by the claws of the evergreen bush. Bobby looked down at his streaked arm and nodded his head. "Is that all that hurts?" Dad said, and the boy nodded again. Now his crying consisted mostly of shudders and little sucks for air.

"I'm going to call Dr. Kinney," Mom said, rising and brushing grass from her knees. "You can run him down there for a quick look, just to make sure he's OK."

Connie looked around at each of us, as if she had forgotten why we were there, and said, "I don't have the car. Robert has it today."

Dad said he thought the boy was just fine, but a doctor's visit wouldn't hurt anything. He would take them in the

DeSoto. "Let me have him while you get dressed," he told Connie. He lifted Bobby from her arms, brushing across her breasts with the back of his hand as he scooped up the child. No one seemed to notice, except me. Mom went in to make the call to the doctor's office, and Connie stood up, adjusting the back of her creeping swimsuit and brushing dirt and grass from her thighs. She touched the back of Bobby's head gently one more time before going into her house to change.

Mom and I were in the dining room setting out sandwiches for just the two of us by the time they loaded the car. We could see the street in front of the Matthewses' house through our dining room window. Dad parked the DeSoto at the curb out front and held the door for Connie while she bent down to arrange Bobby in the seat. She wore a short terry cloth pullover dress now, cinched neatly at the waist with a red belt. As she stood up and turned, my father's hand guided her at the waist as if to steady her, touching her just at the belt. She smiled up at him and said something, reaching up with her own hand and flicking something from his hair, just above his ear. They both laughed, and it was then that I remembered who I was watching. There was just something in the way they looked at each other, as if they were trying too hard not to be nervous, and when he dropped his hand from her hip, it was like the driving of a nail, so natural and so startling I almost made a noise. I looked over at Mom, and she was watching the same thing. She sat and stared out the window for a moment, even after the car doors had slammed and the DeSoto had pulled away from the curb. Suddenly, she tapped the table with her hands, a little drum roll the way Dad did sometimes, and pushed my sandwich toward me.

"I think he's fine, you know," she said. "I think everything is going to be all right."

And he was all right. Just a few scratches and bruises. But for a long time after the day of Bobby's fall, things seemed muddy at our house. There was a thickness that made it hard to walk from room to room, and there was polite conversation in complete sentences where, before the fall, there would have been silence. Things were off beat. They were not copacetic. Eventually, the summer and the patio parties ended, and people seemed to disappear for the winter, emerging at Christmas for eggnog and caroling, then disappearing once again until spring—and a new decade. There was some crying in the spring, and there were nights when the lights in our house stayed on until dawn. My parents began to look older.

That summer, Robert and Connie Matthews moved to Iowa—to a tenure track position at a larger state college. The Nurskis, a retired couple, moved into the Matthewses' house, and the following summer, Dad helped Mr. Nurski build a carport at the side of their house. By then Dad had stopped playing the drums. My left hand had become quicker than his. My solos were more crisp, just a little more complicated, and it made me smile a smile to myself that felt guilty but good, as if he deserved to be left behind. Eventually, on occasion, my father's hands would make my mother laugh again as he spun her toward him. Less got accomplished, though, and they seldom touched. There was a lack of rhythm and joy. Sometimes, mitered corners didn't quite meet.

I was in my second year of college in Lincoln, Nebraska, when my mother called me one cold February morning. It was still dark, and it took me several rings to find the phone.

"I'm sorry, Johnny," she said. "Did I wake you?"

I was still half asleep, so I said the first thing that popped into my head. "No, that's OK. I had to get up to answer the phone anyway." She didn't laugh, and then I knew something was wrong.

After a moment's pause, she just came right out with it, in a quivering but remarkably calm voice. She said that Dad had died in the middle of the night, at the same hospital where I was conceived, and where I was born, and where my mother's minister had tried to take her away from us years before. She talked right through my moans and gasps for breath. There had been an accident at the plant, something about one of the paper-cutting machines not working right. They're supposed to be fixed so the blade won't come down unless your hands are out of the way. Something happened, though, and his hands weren't out of the way, and by the time they got him to the hospital he had lost too much blood. She asked if I could please get someone to drive me home, and I did.

Six months after Dad died, my mother went to work as a secretary for a law firm, and I went back to school. At first, she didn't like it, and she didn't like her boss, the only woman partner in the firm. Her boss, Gail, was just a few years older than Mom, and she would stand in the middle of her office sometimes, shaking with anger, spewing forth four-letter words, and saying things that my mother hated, like "If we lose this motion, I swear I'm going to hang myself." Eventually, though, they became accustomed to one another and, finally, they became friends. Mom still lives in the house in St. Joseph, there in the shadow of King Hill, and she goes dancing in Kansas City once in a while with a lawyer she met there during the course of some litigation. She travels a fair bit and eats in fine restaurants.

I live in North Carolina now, where my wife and I are painters. We paint the mountains and quiet, small-town street scenes, and our paintings sell for surprisingly large sums. My wife does wonderful things with light, much bolder things than I do. We have a six-year-old son, and sometimes his hands remind me of my father's. I can already tell that his hands will be larger than mine. A hammer fits there. He swings it well. My wife loves to see that, and she loves to hold him in her lap and whisper things to him. I can tell by her eyes that she thinks he will be the one—the one to whom secrets must be revealed, the one who will be at home with both the softness and boldness of light. He'll be the one who can keep things from breaking. I suppose we both have hope.

I talk to Mom some on the phone, although not very much. At times, it's as if something has been given up between us without a specific precipitating event. Maybe it's nothing more than time and distance. Maybe it's just that the hope of things wears off once a son becomes just another man. Mom never told me anything about Dad and Connie Matthews, but she didn't really have to. I know, but I don't know—not the specifics anyway. Mom has never offered a story about what was going on in their lives at that time, and I'm not sure that I would have accepted it the way she might have offered it. I think I would understand some of it now, though—now that I'm a little older than he was then—now that I know a little something about his short, rhymeless life poem, and about days of tears and nights when the lights don't go out. For my dad, maybe it didn't have much to do with Connie Matthews or my mother. Maybe it had something to do with his hands starting to lose their grip. Maybe it was about gravity, and how it slows us down and how we fool ourselves into thinking we need to fight it—that we need to clutch at things before they slip through our fingers. We try to take, and grasp, and hold. It's an expanding universe, though, and things fly away. Sometimes it leaves us weak.

But my mother has never offered me a story about my father's fight with gravity. When we do talk, though, she is generous with news and stories about her new life, and she still tells me things that surprise me sometimes, not so much from the content but from the effect. Like the last time we talked. Right before we hung up, she told me a joke about four cars that came to an intersection all at the same time. One car was driven by Santa Claus, one was driven by the Easter Bunny, one was driven by a perfect man, and one was driven by a perfect woman. So who had the right-of-way? I told her I didn't know, and she said, of course, it was the woman. Everybody knows the other three are just make-believe. I didn't really feel like laughing at the punch line, and maybe she didn't really expect me to, but I did anyway.

"That's good," I told her. "That was a good one." That's all I could think of to say, even though I didn't really think it. I couldn't think of a way to tell her how far from funny I thought that joke was, or how hurtful it can be for some men to realize how imperfect they are. There's just no telling how great the disappointment can be sometimes when we find out that we will never be able to keep up with Gene Krupa, or when we discover that our all too human hands can give us away—by making the illusion of Santa Claus incomplete and by causing pain to those we never meant to hurt. And that all seems startling and sad to me right now, as I watch my wife and my own son holding each other and laughing wildly at something I have just missed by stepping away from them for only a moment.

Short-Term Losses

LLOYD CHRISTENSEN eased the long Mercury into the parking space a few rows down from the snack bar. The sun was just disappearing behind the long stockade fence that separated the drive-in theater from the heavy traffic of the Belt highway. He was too far away from the speaker at first, so he backed up to try again. The next time, he cramped the wheels too much, and the passenger door of the Mercury was right up next to the metal pole with the speakers. His wife, Lois, wouldn't be able to get in or out with the pole that close, so he started to back up again.

"This is all right, Lloyd," his wife said. "Just leave it. With your eyesight, we'll be here all night just trying to get parked."

"You can't get out," he said. "What if you need to use the restroom or something?"

"You're the one with the prostate trouble, not me," she said. "I'll be fine. And if I need anything to eat, I'll just send you."

"Do you trust me to make it back?" Lloyd asked.

"You'll be fine," she said. "For crying out loud, the snack bar is only a few rows away."

Lois's attitude toward Lloyd's short-term memory loss fluctuated. Sometimes she was tolerant and sometimes she was impatient. When he first developed the problem, about six years after he retired from the railroad and about two years after his prostate went bad, Lois was irritated. It was as if she thought he was doing it on purpose, just to confuse and embarrass her in public. They would be out shopping, become separated, and Lloyd would get lost. He wouldn't remember what store they had been in or where he had parked the car. They went to a neurologist after the third time Lois had to have shopping center security guards help her find him.

"Short-term memory loss is fairly common among men your age," the doctor had told him. "You know, getting up there in years. You'll probably notice that your long-term memory isn't affected—probably even be able to remember things about when you were a kid, but you might not remember what you had for breakfast an hour ago."

Even after the talk with the doctor, though, Lois still acted for a time as if he could control it—that he really could remember if he wanted to—and that he was just being hard to get along with.

"It's just so frustrating," she would say. "You used to wander away on purpose. Now you wander away by accident. What am I supposed to think?"

Lloyd and Lois sat in the bluish dusk of the drive-in theater waiting for it to get dark enough for the movies to begin. There was a double feature of old Hitchcock films—*The Man Who Knew Too Much* and *Rear Window*. Lloyd had always liked Jimmy Stewart and was flattered once in a while when someone would mention that he resembled the movie star. He supposed the resemblance was greater in recent years, when they had both become "elderly" as well as tall and thin.

Above the screen, pinpoint stars were beginning to appear in the purple sky that had settled in over northwest Missouri. Below the screen, a group of children played on the playground equipment in the fenced play area at the front of the theater, an area that was lighted like a stage by large floodlights mounted along the top of the tall, gray-white screen.

"Watch me, watch this!" the children squealed to their chatting parents. Little girls skinned the cat and boys with holes in their jeans tried to run back up the slide without using the ladder. "Hop down, I'll catch you," a father said to a child on the jungle gym. The trusting child stepped out into air, laughing, without hesitating. The father pulled the child gently to his chest and to the ground. They walked hand in hand back to their car to wait for the cartoons. It was almost dark enough.

"Remember when the girls were that little?" Lloyd asked. He nodded toward the playground.

"Sometimes it's hard," Lois said.

"I wish Joyce would bring the kids around more often," he said, his jaw tightening. "It's not as if she lives in Oregon like her sister."

"She comes by every week," Lois said. "Besides, when she was there so much last summer, when you were sick, the kids nearly drove you crazy." She patted his thin leg. "Joyce is a good girl. She does a lot for us."

"She doesn't really like to, though," he said, "especially for me." He stared at the blank screen. "I can tell. She just does it because she feels obligated."

"Oh, just stop it," Lois said. "Stop feeling sorry for yourself." It was dark now and they were silent. Whiffs of hot grease and popcorn drifted up from the snack bar.

Lloyd was able to put off a visit to the restroom until the point in the first movie where Jimmy Stewart and Doris Day had flown to London in search of Ambrose Chapel. He remembered what happened next anyway—Jimmy Stewart would go to a taxidermist shop by mistake.

"Prostate's got the best of me," Lloyd said. "Do you want anything from the snack bar while I'm up there?"

"I'll take a hot dog and iced tea. But look around first and try to remember where the car is parked."

Lloyd looked around again and saw the playground in front and the snack bar lights to the rear a few rows back. He walked slowly along the narrow sidewalk that was lined with dim, low footlights. The walkway was covered with scattered gravel that rolled under his feet like marbles spilled from a jar, and he had to concentrate hard on not losing his footing.

He found the restroom and then the snack bar. They both had long lines. Behind the counter at the snack bar was a dwarf man, or a midget—Lloyd wasn't sure about the difference—but he thought this man was a dwarf because he was so stocky and had nubby, fat fingers and bowed legs. His small feet shuffled in quick little hop-steps as he moved back and forth behind the counter, pouring soft drinks and spearing hot dogs and shouting orders through a window into the kitchen. His voice was surprisingly deep.

Lloyd watched the dwarf closely while he waited for the slow line to move forward. He was intrigued by his quick movements and all the extra effort the small man had to make to accomplish simple tasks. There were stepstools placed at strategic places behind the counter and the dwarf bobbed up and down, on and off the stools, appearing and disappearing at the countertop.

"What'll it be?" the dwarf boomed when Lloyd reached the front of the line. He hesitated, then remembered what he wanted to order. The dwarf put the drinks and foil-wrapped food in a cardboard tray, and Lloyd backed out of the exit into darkness and onto another slippery, gravel-covered sidewalk. He was still thinking about the quick dwarf and the rolling gravel under his feet as he walked away from the yellow lights of the snack bar. He walked for what he thought should be a sufficient distance away from the lights, stood between a row of cars, and turned in circles looking for his Mercury. He didn't notice that the screen was much smaller than it had been before he went to the restroom. He walked farther down the sidewalk, away from the screen, and the rows of cars became darker and darker. His knees felt weak.

When he came to the back of the theater, there were rows of vans and pickup trucks parked backwards, with their tailgates facing the screen. Some of the vans were painted in glowing colors, with pictures of muscular men and horses with flowing manes and partially nude women, and most of the trucks had Japanese names and sat high up off the ground on large balloon tires.

"Hey, Grandpa, are ya lost?" one of the boys in the back of a pickup truck yelled. Some of the older kids in the truck snorted and giggled and said something that Lloyd couldn't hear. There were boys and girls in the truck, some of them lying down. The boy who yelled sat on top of a Coors cooler and was sipping from a can.

"Nope, I'm not lost," Lloyd said. "Just stretching some stiff legs." Even as he said it, he knew he should have ignored them.

"Yeah, they look pretty stiff all right," the boy with the beer said. "Looks like you're about ready to go to stiff city there, Gramps." The kids in the truck laughed out loud.

"Damn kids," Lloyd mumbled as he walked away.

When he was almost to the next row of cars, a half-empty beer can thudded behind him in the gravel and splashed his cuffs and shoes with beer. He didn't turn but just kept walking toward the screen, his face flushed with anger and embarrassment, so the veins in his nose stood out in blue streaks. "Damn kids," he mumbled again and looked up at the screen.

Suddenly he was even more confused. He stood in the dark, blinking up at the lighted movements of the characters; but instead of Jimmy Stewart and Doris Day, he saw himself and his friends as boys. And he saw old Josh Streeter. Their images spun and shimmered and then locked into place on the screen only for an instant. It was just long enough for Lloyd to see the boys running—long enough to see they were stealing something from an injured old man.

Lloyd wobbled to a stop after what he thought was a few seconds and craned his head around. His hands shook and the cardboard tray with the snack bar food began to collapse. His mind and feet had wandered for some time, and now he found himself standing behind another row of strange, darkened cars. Up on the screen, Doris Day was at Albert Hall and the orchestra was beginning to warm up. He felt light-headed and needed to sit or lean on something. The blood pulsed in his neck and pinpoint flashes of light danced in front of him in the dark. He was somewhere near the middle of the theater, but as he walked and walked along the row of cars, he couldn't find the sidewalk that would take him to the distant lights of the snack bar. He didn't want to walk between the cars because he didn't want to have to bend low under each of the speaker wires.

He shuffled along behind a row of cars. In the cars were

children who leaned sleeping against the back doors or were draped over the front seats between their parents. Young mothers nibbled at popcorn and fathers sat hunched down behind the steering wheels or with one arm resting outstretched along the tops of the bench seats. Some of them flipped cigarette ashes out the windows.

Lloyd walked until he started to have trouble breathing. He stopped and sucked deeply, trying to fill each cubic inch of his lungs with oxygen, but his lungs wouldn't be satisfied. His throat constricted briefly in the drowning panic of not being able to pull in enough air, and Lloyd grabbed the back of a nearby car. He concentrated on taking slow, even breaths until the panic passed.

The couple in the car didn't even notice him. The young man, maybe in his thirties, glared straight ahead over the steering wheel, but his eyes weren't focused on the screen. The young woman sat far over in her corner of the car with her shoulders turned away from the man. She stared out the passenger window. Her eyes were moist and she didn't look at the young man when she spoke.

"I trusted you," she said faintly through the open window. The young man said nothing in defense. "I've always trusted you," she said, "and now it all comes out."

"I told you, it didn't mean anything," the young man said. "It's got nothing to do with us—it's just something that happened."

"You mean it's just something that I happened to find out about," she said, turning toward him. "Jeez, Bobby, how can you sit there and—damn you." Her face was streaked wet now, but she smiled faintly and shook her head. "You know, the thing is, if you were going to do something like this, you could have done a lot better than her."

The young man leaned his head back against the seat,

stared down his nose at the screen, and was silent. The woman turned toward her window again, sobbing silently and biting at her lower lip.

Lloyd moved away from the back of the car. Up on the screen, the Albert Hall orchestra was building toward a crescendo. He walked for a short distance and his chest tightened; he became confused again, disoriented. The music grew louder and he looked up at the screen. But now he didn't see Albert Hall. What was it? Now he saw the old Cowtown Bar and Grill and, instead of an orchestra, he heard the pounding and country twang of Darrell Carol and his Cracker Barrel Band. The scene spun and locked into place on the screen.

Lloyd was a young man and he stood at the dark bar in his railroad coveralls and flannel shirt. Tinsel and glass ornaments and streamers hung from the walls and from the bar. Lloyd and his friends from the rail yard smoked heavily and squinted at each other through the dense air as they drank beer and laughed and cursed the bad weather and lack of money. Moose Downs, the owner of the Cowtown, tended bar and wore a false white beard and a floppy red hat. It was Christmas Eve of 1938—the one that Lloyd spent in jail—just before he and Lois split up for a time and almost divorced.

"Why in the hell aren't you boys home with your families?" Moose yelled over the loud fiddle music. "Don't you have some bicycles or wagons or something to put together?"

"Oh, it'll get done, Moose old buddy," Lloyd said. "Just keep a few more of those beers coming. I'm getting primed for some real creative bicycle construction tonight." Lloyd and his friends laughed hard and coughed and slapped each other on their backs.

They had been drinking for some time when Angel Rock came into the bar. Angel was a barmaid there part-time and would come into the Cowtown even on her nights off to dance and cuss with the boys at the bar. Lloyd was attracted to her in a way that was confusing. She wasn't as attractive as Lois, maybe a little older and certainly a little heavier. Angel wasn't fat necessarily—there was just something about her figure that reminded Lloyd of a bowling pin—and she had blonde hair that wasn't really blonde.

"Merry Christmas, boys!" Angel shrieked as she pounded snow from her shoes. "Ho, Ho, Ho!"

"I always knew you were a big Ho," one of the boys from the rail yard yelled. Everyone, even Angel, laughed.

"Well, hell yes," Angel snorted. "Isn't this a Ho house?" Everyone laughed even louder and a couple of the men at the bar called to Moose to set Angel up with a drink. She drank with the men and one other woman who was there for a while, then she eased in next to Lloyd at the bar and spoke softly.

"Lloyd old boy, I'm glad you're here tonight. I've got a little Christmas present for you out in my car." Her eyes were glazed and when she smiled in close to Lloyd's face, he could smell the sweet taint of liquor and perfumed makeup. Her skin was porous, even through the heavy makeup, and heat passed through her tight red Christmas sweater.

"Well, I'm glad you thought of me, Angel," Lloyd said, smiling stupidly. His head hummed from the beer and smoke. "But we talked about this. You and me have to call it quits. I need to think about Lois and the kids."

"Now, Lloyd old boy, don't get yourself all worked up.

I'm just talking about going out to the car and having a little snort of some really fine bourbon—not like this monkey piss Moose serves."

"Well, maybe just for a drink. I gotta go soon."

"Sure," she said. "Come on out for a drink of that smooth bourbon. We'll drink a toast to the season—to Lois and those girls of yours." She put her hand on his hip to nudge him toward the door.

They went into the night air and snow without jackets, leaning on each other and weaving. They were just bending to get in Angel's car when Lois pulled in beside them. She rolled down her window but didn't turn off the car engine.

"It's almost midnight on Christmas Eve," Lois said through clenched teeth. "Were you going to come home sometime tonight?"

"Lois, we were just . . ."

"I think I see what you were just up to," Lois said, her voice shaking. "I put the girls to bed by myself tonight. I guess I can wake them by myself in the morning—so don't bother coming home." She tried to roll the window up and drive away at the same time, letting the clutch out too fast and almost killing the engine. "I'm through trusting you," she said, and the window closed.

"Wait, Lois, I was just getting ready to go!" he yelled and ran after her. She spun out of the parking lot and threw back slush and gravel that stung Lloyd's cheeks. He ran back to Angel's car and hopped in, fishtailing out of the lot. Angel ran after him yelling.

"You come back with that car! You're too drunk to drive!"

She ran out into the street and stood beneath the dim streetlight, feet spread, holding a bottle of bourbon by the neck and cursing at Lloyd as he drove her car out of sight into a lace curtain of snowflakes that twirled toward her out of the darkness. In a few seconds, she heard the dull thud and tinkle of breaking glass in the distance, where Lloyd had run her car into a snowbank, and where he still sat when the police came.

Lloyd had hoped they would keep him jailed all day so he would have an excuse for not facing Lois. But in a show of great magnanimity, the sheriff released all of the prisoners from the drunk tank by midmorning on Christmas.

He had forgotten that he didn't have his coat until the taxi let him out in front of his house. He trembled with the chill and his head pounded; each step toward the front door was an effort. Even though he could tell the sun was well up in the overcast sky, the window blinds were still drawn on most of the houses up and down his street. Everyone would still be milling around in their pajamas, opening presents and having their third, maybe fourth, cup of coffee. He reached for the doorknob, then stopped and sat in the porch swing. He sat hunched forward, with his knees together, blowing into his cupped hands to bring sensation back into his fingertips. He could hear the girls, Joyce and Margie, laughing and running through the house. Christmas gift squeals. He could hear Lois, though he couldn't make out what she was saying, and her voice sounded level and calm—no screeching edges that betrayed pain.

It was true, he thought. She could take care of herself, and they were perfectly happy to have Christmas without him. He shook, at first, he thought, because of the cold; then he shook harder and harder with anger at not being missed more profoundly.

He heard Lois laugh. He got up and walked back down the sidewalk trying to stay in the same blue-shadowed footprints he had made in the snow when he came up the walk.

He marched off into the snow like an offended demigod, for whom these worshipers' sacrifices weren't enough. He just kept going and didn't come back for almost three months.

He could see it all clearly now, as if it were a home movie being played back for a visiting relative. Lois whimpering under the covers at night. Joyce biting her fingernails. Margie wetting the bed again. But there were gaps. He wasn't sure what brought them together again and held them. Loneliness. Finances maybe. The girls. That part of it was unclear.

But when Lois had taken him back, she said, "Things can never be the same. Maybe, someday, it will be close. But things can never be quite the same between us. Do you understand, Lloyd Christensen?"

Her saying his full name, Lloyd Christensen, was like an incantation. It was as if by just saying the name out loud she was able to capture some unintelligible essence of him and clasp it to her breast so that he couldn't—didn't want to—escape. She was a shaman in an ancient rite, and he would atone. There was some occasional backsliding, though—still too many lies and too many tears that could have been avoided. Lloyd could see that now.

"Lloyd Christensen," a deep voice boomed. The sound seemed all around him, rumbling and resonant. Lloyd stiffened, then almost collapsed with weakness, blinking back tears. The floodlights above the screen were just a glare through his fogged glasses and the deep voice shook him again like a call from beyond.

"Lloyd Christensen, please report to the snack bar. Your wife is waiting." It was the dwarf's voice and it was coming out over the public address system. It also came out of each little speaker attached to each car in the theater, so Lloyd was surrounded by the echo of his name.

The movie was over and the screen was lighted once again by the humming, overhanging lamps that resembled streetlights. To his right, and nearby now, was the snack bar. He moved stiffly, the ball and socket of his hip and the floating discs of his spine scraping and grating as he limped toward the yellow string of lights that lined the roof of the snack bar. He bent low to duck under speaker wires, inching between cars and almost falling twice. Lois saw him and walked as briskly as she could toward him, her shoulders dipping from side to side in an arthritic lope that favored her frozen right knee and hip. She saw he was near collapse and supported him at the elbows when he reached to embrace her. The dwarf stood behind her in the doorway looking on, his arms akimbo.

"You see there, Mrs. Christensen, I told you he'd show up," the dwarf said. "You gave her a little scare there, Lloyd." The dwarf stood smiling, a big silver tooth shining in front.

"I'm sorry," Lloyd said into her shoulder. "I'm so sorry for everything." His voice cracked and failed, clogged with phlegm.

"It's all right," she said, patting his shoulder as if he were an infant. "You can't help it when these things happen. I understand that now."

"No, it's not that," he said.

"Hush, now," she said. "Let's get you back to the car. You can hardly walk." They walked slowly, both limping, with their arms looped around each other's waist.

Lloyd glanced around furtively as they walked toward the Mercury. He had the vague feeling that people were watching him, that they knew he was having trouble, and he noticed for the first time that many of the cars around them contained older couples, some of them elderly. He slid across into the passenger's seat and hunched down, his long legs pulled in tight beneath the dashboard.

He rocked back and forth and shook quietly, wiping his face with the back of his crinkled, purple-spotted hand. Lois held tight to the steering wheel and watched, her mouth opening once or twice to speak; she hesitated, looked away and then looked back at Lloyd. She reached tentatively and touched his arm lightly. "It's all right, Lloyd. You don't have to be ashamed. You just forget, that's all."

He looked up pleadingly, wringing his hands in his lap. "That's not it," he said. "I'm sorry. Please forgive me. I haven't forgotten." His face contorted and he looked away. He stared at the blank screen.

"Of course you forgot. You just forget for a little while. It'll come back to you."

"No, no, no, no!" he moaned in a long, low whine that rose almost to a keen. He pounded his folded hands in his lap and rocked forward and back and wept openly for all the things he remembered, not the things he forgot. He cried for all the little perjuries and petty larcenies of his life and for all the pain that had been absorbed by those whom he had loved not quite enough. Lois sat with her mouth open as he wept into his hands. She offered her hand again and he pressed it to his moist face.

He looked up again at Lois and then stared for a moment at the big, blank screen. Some of the young parents had taken their children back down to the lighted playground again during the intermission. Maybe a dozen children ran through the sand and squealed and climbed over the equipment. And there was another child high up on the jungle gym, whose father stood below and clapped his hands and yelled, "Jump down, honey. I'll catch you." The child, a little girl with a ponytail, leaned forward, smiling.

Lloyd saw himself again, as if in a movie. He was the child high up in the air beneath the bright lights. Below was blackness, but he felt no fear. He hesitated only for a moment, then smiled and jumped off into the open arms of dark eternity, not knowing if he could ever come back, but trusting he would be caught.

Failing To Close

July 15

Dear Zeke,
 Your widow has moved back to California, and I'm selling our parents' house. I assume you know Dad and Mom were killed. Maybe that's assuming too much—that you would know all about the comings and goings of the dead. I just thought I'd keep you posted about things of this earth, but maybe I should bring you up to date on things not of this earth, so you won't be confused by missing names or gaps in the news.
 For about a year after you were killed, Mom and Dad just seemed to go through the motions of living—slow motions punctuated with fits of crying and something that might best be described as petit mal seizures. They were like trances of grief, and they scared the hell out of me. It was as if they were with you for a few seconds, as if they had passed beyond the pale, so to speak, then they would return to us, wet-eyed. They said they were just sad, absent-minded. But

I could tell they had been somewhere. Then Dad decided they should take a trip—get away from the business for a while, take their minds off things. He decided they should go to Florida.

It was November and starting to get cold here in Missouri, so they thought Key West would be just the thing. So did Lisa. She encouraged them, but I was against it. There was just something about it that made me uncomfortable. But you know Lisa. (I guess you should—you were married to her.) She thought it was a good idea and got all enthusiastic in that manic way she has about her, and the whole thing just steamrolled until there was no stopping them.

"Oh, John," Lisa would say to me, "you are absolutely macabre with these weird feelings you have." She pronounced macabre as if it rhymed with sabre. Anyway, she would tell me, "They are not going to be killed. They are not subconsciously trying to follow Zeke into death."

Well, little brother, to make a long story short, I was right and Lisa was wrong. You see, there was this drunk driver vacationing there—from Spokane, I think. Anyway, Mom and Dad were standing on the sidewalk at this little outdoor market, and, well—I suppose they never knew what hit them. That's the part I thought you probably already knew about, and I don't want to talk about it. But that's why I had to move back here from Kansas City—to take care of the house and the business. I sold off my shares in the business (what's a thirty-seven-year-old, long-haired, bearded law professor going to do with a tractor and farm implement dealership?) and, as I said, I'm selling the house. It went on the market last week. It's mostly empty already. I have a bed set up in the dining room and a table and chair set up in the kitchen. In the refrigerator, I have milk, beer, bread, and a carton of cigarettes—four of my five major food groups. And on the kitchen table, I have the computer on which I'm writing.

The rest of the house is empty. Remember the front hall? The polished oak floor that goes along the stairway and into the kitchen? It's newly waxed and polished. This evening, before I sat down to write to you, I put on a fresh pair of white socks and ran and slid up and down the hallway, from the front door to the kitchen counter. It's a straight shot now. No rugs or tables in the way. You can really get up a head of steam and slide on that floor now, Zeke.

You might like the house empty like this. The acoustics are great—twelve large, empty rooms of high ceilings, hardwood and tile floors, and rock 'n' roll. I forgot to mention, I have a tape player, too. So I have a bed, food, cigarettes, a computer, and music. I play some of your old tapes sometimes. Did I ever mention how good you were? Did you really know how to sing and play the guitar like that, or does the sixteen-track recording system just make it seem that way? Anyway, sometimes I play your tapes—to hear your voice. But then I switch back to Van Morrison or Eric Clapton. I can turn "Layla" up as loud as I want to.

Anyway, as I started to say, Lisa has moved back to California. I guess she felt she was to blame somehow, just because she encouraged Mom and Dad to take the trip, and I think the strain on her explains some of her behavior lately. It started last winter, after the crash, when Lisa was living here at the house. She was trying to be helpful, I think. I was left alone to take care of all this stuff, you see, and so we agreed that she would live here because I had to stay in Kansas City to teach my classes. I just felt like someone needed to be here to keep an eye on things through the winter. Water pipes, gas furnace—that sort of thing. There was tension between us, though. She wouldn't smile, and she seemed weighed down by me when I would check in on her, as if I did it just to find fault.

I swear, Zeke, I never criticized her at all. But she said she could just tell, by the tone of my voice and the way I screwed up my eyebrows, that I disapproved of the way she did things. She didn't take care of the house very well, though. I have to admit that. But I swear, I never criticized her. Just suggested things she could do differently, like not leaving garbage all over the kitchen or letting her Labrador live in the house day and night. I told her that accounted for the smell and that it would make it hard to show the house when I put it on the market. She cried and said that I had never liked her. I told her that wasn't true.

Then, this spring, Ira Kurzbaum called me while I was in Kansas City. Remember Mr. Kurzbaum, Mom and Dad's neighbor? He called, very flustered. He said he hated to bother me with such things, but Mrs. Kurzbaum was making him call. "She's running around the backyard without anything on," he said.

"Who? Mrs. Kurzbaum?"

"No! That woman at your parents' house, your sister-in-law."

"Lisa? What do you mean, exactly?"

"Out by the pool in the backyard, John. She swims, lies in the sun, you know? No clothes."

"How do you know?"

"The fence isn't that high!"

"Has anyone complained?"

"Mrs. Kurzbaum! Mrs. Kurzbaum is complaining. She's complaining to me every day that I should do something about it, so I'm calling you. It's your house now."

It was raining when I went to see her at the house. It was raining hard, too. And there was your Mustang sitting in the driveway with the top down, taking on quarts of water. The inside was soaked. I put the top up, then I yelled in through the front door to see if Lisa was there. No answer.

I stepped into the front hall and yelled, "Lisa?" Still nothing, but I thought I heard some noise coming from the kitchen, so I walked in that direction.

"Did you know your car top was down?" I said.

When I came to the kitchen doorway, I could see Lisa with her back to me, moving back and forth at the counter and wearing a Walkman headset. She had a tiny tape player slung around her hips with a thin black string, with the wire to the headset snaking up her back and over her shoulder. Other than that, though, she wasn't wearing anything. I'm embarrassed, Zeke, but she was absolutely naked, and she was just dancing around the kitchen that way, pouring milk into a bowl of Froot Loops cereal and popping the top on a Diet Coke. She was tan all over. I tried to look past her, at the wall, at the floor, at something. My face was burning red through my beard. And I knew I'd scare the shit out of her if I tried to get her attention. I didn't know what to do.

I was just thinking about leaving, sneaking back out and trying all over again, when she swung around toward the refrigerator with the milk and saw me. She screamed like she'd touched high voltage, and the milk carton went splat on the floor. It landed right-side-up, and only a little milk squirted out of the top. Don't you think that's really lucky?

Anyway, I took a step toward her, my palms raised to try to calm her, to show I didn't have any weapons. "Lisa, it's me!" I said. "I didn't mean to scare you!"

She ripped the earphones from her head, backing toward the corner where the cabinets and the wall meet, trembling and cursing like a sailor.

"Jesus H. Christ, John!" she yelled. "You nearly gave me

a fucking heart attack!" She was caught somewhere between crying and laughing, and she tried to turn her shoulders and pelvis away from me, crossing her arms and offering me a view of her rear rather than her front. I just thought you should know that, Zeke.

"Look," I said. "How about if I go back out in the other room and wait for you to go put some clothes on? We need to talk."

"Fine," she said, still turned away from me. "So go!"

I went back out to the front hall, and she flashed past me and up the stairs in a blur of bare legs and feet. She was only gone a few minutes, and when she came back down, she was wearing jeans and a white T-shirt.

She went right past me and back out to the kitchen, busying herself with cleaning up the dropped milk and rearranging her bowl of cereal at the table.

"Sorry about the little scene there," she said, still red and still not looking straight at me. "I just haven't been out of the house yet today."

"So is that the only time you put on clothes now?"

"Well, they'd arrest me if I didn't, don't you think?" She sat down at the table to eat her cereal. "I'm sorry if you're really uptight about it. Zeke and I used to go that way all the time at home, and I still do it sometimes."

"Well, this isn't exactly your home, and I'm not nearly as uptight about it as the neighbors are."

"So that's it," she said, putting her spoon down. "That's what you wanted to talk about? I wondered when the old lady was going to complain. I swear, every time that old goat next door hears a splash in the pool over here, he finds some excuse to get out in the yard and putter around."

"I don't know about that," I said. I was standing in the kitchen doorway again. "But I do know the Kurzbaums have been good neighbors for years, and we're not going to have this shit."

"Oh, so we're not going to have this shit! Is that right?" She pushed herself away from the table. "Fine! You take care of this damn house! You criticize everything I do anyway. I'm going back to California. I can wear whatever I damn well please there, do whatever I please and not have to answer to Mr. Professor."

"That's right!" I said, turning red again. "You go do what you want, go wear what you want, snort what you want up your fucking nose and kill yourself just like him!"

She stood up and balanced the bowl of cereal in her right hand, feet planted, chest out, just like a quarterback, and threw the bowl at me as hard as she could. It crashed against the wall, right behind my ear, and sprayed pastel milk all over the hallway. "You son of a bitch!" she screamed. "I knew it! I knew you blamed me for that. Just like you blame me for your Mom and Dad, too!" She stood, clenching and unclenching her fists, heaving and crying. She looked as if she would say something else, but instead, she crossed her arms in front of her, turned from me with her head lowered, and sobbed.

I thought about it for just a moment—just a few heartbeats—then I said, "I don't blame you for Zeke. Look, I'm sorry. I'll take care of the house, okay? Maybe you should go back to California. It's what you're used to now. This is like a mausoleum around here."

"I'm not to blame," she said and ran out of the room.

That's been about two months ago. She drove the Mustang all the way to California by herself. Her and the Labrador. Said she isn't going to fly anymore—something about life being too risky. She sent me a card after she arrived. All it said was: "I'm here. Doing much better. Take care of yourself, Lisa." I don't know how it will turn out with her, Zeke. Maybe you know already. I hope she'll be all right. I swear, I didn't blame her for anything. Well, maybe I did, but I didn't really say it out loud. I'm sorry, Zeke. Maybe you know all this already. I miss you.

Love,
John

JULY 20

Dear Zeke,

No lookers for the house yet. I don't expect it to move very quickly. The economy around here isn't great anymore, and there are several other houses in the neighborhood for sale.

In fact, something has come up with Mrs. Waisbloom's house over on Hall Street. Remember? The huge brick and sandstone Victorian place on the corner? Spires, turrets, terra-cotta trim, parquet floors, stained glass windows. She has the carriage house out back where you kissed her niece once. Anyway, she signed a contract with a buyer, and now she wants out of it. She's asked me to help her. I told her I do constitutional law, that I don't know much about property transactions, but that I'd see what I can do. So that's the other thing I'm doing in my spare time, besides writing to you.

I don't know much about this after-life or telepathy jazz either, but, just in case, I thought it would be best to do this on the computer. It's just a vague notion I have about neurons, synapses, on-off, yes-no, microcircuits, Mary Shelley, and all that. I'm not going to bother printing any of this out. If you don't pick it up directly from the hard disk somehow, then it probably won't get there—I'm pretty sure there's not a modem for this sort of thing.

Anyway, the thing about Mrs. Waisbloom's house is that she decided she doesn't like the people who were going to buy it. I'm not sure that that's a valid reason for rescinding a sales contract, but that's her reason—she doesn't like them. She's getting very frail. You might remember she was always small and seemed to be lost in that huge house of hers. Her health is failing her now, though. Something about her blood pressure jumping up and down. Her mind is still sharp, though, and she still plays the role of the venerated physician's wife to the hilt—rectitude personified.

"I just will not sell to those people," she told me. "They are absolutely vulgar." She's telling me this as I'm sitting in her kitchen sipping tea in my long hair and jeans with holes in the knees. Apparently she isn't perplexed about a strange youth growing into a strange adult.

I told her they sounded like they would be very attractive buyers. He's the new president of the Wire and Cable Company.

"They're from the East," she said. "They're just not like us."

Their names are Fitzpatrick and they come from Boston. She told me all about their first meeting. Michael Fitzpatrick is big and blustery, with a shock of white hair and a raspy, saw-toothed voice. His wife is almost as large, grossly overweight, and, to hear Mrs. Waisbloom tell it, she was absolutely intoxicated the morning they came to look at the house. They have a teenage son, Jimmy, I think, who is large and soft and pimply.

"The first thing in the door," Mrs. Waisbloom said, "their son said the house smelled funny, that it smelled like sick, old people. He said it smelled like dead bodies!"

"Maybe you didn't hear him correctly," I said. "Surely, even a kid wouldn't say that."

"Oh, he said it. His father glared at him and told him to shut up, just like that. No apology. Just, shut up. The mother pretended she didn't hear any of it. Then, do you know what the son did?" Mrs. Waisbloom blushed, her hand fluttered at her lips, and she said, "He said the, oh my, the 'F' word, to his father. Right there in my hallway, he said it. Then his father told him to shut up again."

She twisted a small handkerchief in her tiny, thin hands as she told me all this. Then she told me that her regular attorney, Herzel Luckbinder, is on the board at Wire and Cable, and that's why she wanted me to see what I could do about getting out of the sales contract.

"I just can't have those people living here," she said.

So far, I haven't figured out a way for her to get out of the contract. If the Fitzpatricks want it bad enough, they could probably sue for specific performance if Mrs. Waisbloom breaches the agreement. I do have an idea, though. I'll let you know what happens.

Love,
John

JULY 25

Dear Zeke,

I might have the solution. Wait. You don't know what the problem is, do you? Actually, the problem is now threefold. First, Mrs. Waisbloom doesn't want to sell her house to the Fitzpatricks. Second, nobody has even called my broker yet to inquire about this house. She says it's too much house and too pricey for the economy around here, and no new folks with the bucks are moving in—except the Fitzpatricks. So do you get the picture?

I told my broker to tell their broker that Mrs. Waisbloom

might have some trouble closing the sale when the Fitzpatricks wanted to (since "time is of the essence" is not in their contract, technically she wouldn't be in breach if she delayed the closing somewhat), and that they could have possession immediately on this place if they wanted it. I told her to assure them that Mrs. Waisbloom wouldn't make trouble if they pulled out of her contract. They're coming over tomorrow to look this place over. Sounds like the kid really likes the idea of having a pool.

    The tertiary problem is, I don't know what my problem is. I can't work. I'm supposed to be contributing three chapters to a new casebook that West Publishing is putting out, and I can't get anywhere with them. I'm also supposed to be doing an article for the ABA Journal on the October Supreme Court term. Zero. Nothing. When Flaubert was working on *Madame Bovary*, he wrote to a friend, "One week—two pages!" Well, I ain't Flaubert, and "search and seizure" law ain't *Bovary*, but I can't even claim two pages yet. A big zippo. I'm surrounded by boxes of photocopies of cases and law review articles here in the kitchen. I just stare at the boxes and stare at the fluorescent green blip on the screen in front of me, then I get up to get another beer and to go out on the back porch for a smoke—out of habit. Remember how mad Mom would get if we'd light up in the house?

    I moved the bed into our old room, and I was doing this again last night—lying in the dark in our room humming the old TV show tunes. Remember that game? We'd take turns humming the theme song from a TV show, and the other one would guess what show it was from. Remember that? *F Troop. Get Smart. Dick Van Dyke. Mission Impossible.* I've been trying to dredge up some of the tunes from the recesses of this otherwise worthless brain. *Hawaii Five-O* was easy. *Mission Impossible* came pretty quickly. Some of the others, though—they're just gone. I can't get them back and it's driving me crazy—just like when you'd stump me with one and then not tell me the answer, and I would lie there in the dark trying to think of it and be so pissed off at you.

Now, when I can't remember the tunes and I can't remember you very clearly, I get so pissed that I can't sleep. And sometimes when I can't sleep, I'll do this: I'll sit at the kitchen table and unfold my pocketknife—the one with the white pearl handle and the little silver shield on the side. I'll hold the knife in one hand, lay my other arm out along the table, and look for the good veins. The fat blue worms near the wrist roll like restless sleep under the point of the knife. There's a tingle when you apply pressure with the edge of the blade. There's an electric sensation to it, like fluorescent green blips in the blood, something you can feel all the way down to your scrotum and up into your jaw teeth. Very seductive. But then it passes.

Even after bad nights, I have good intentions of getting up early and getting some of this work done. But I usually just roam around the yard for a while with a cup of coffee. Remember how the old man would do that on the weekends? Just roam around with his coffee out in the yard. Did I tell you I went over to the high school the other night to play a little pickup basketball? I'm still not very good. Anyway, things are crumbling a little there—the asphalt is cracked and weeds are growing through the gaps—but the old neighborhood looks pretty much the same. Other parts of town are going to hell in a handbasket, though. Sixth Street, where Dad's tractor dealership is, looks like a war zone.

But I digress. I guess that's my problem. I'm having trouble concentrating. Something is going on. Something is paralyzing me. Right now, though, I think I'll walk to the park. Some of the guys still play cards down there in the evenings. I'll let you know what happens with the Fitzpatricks and the house.

Love,
John

July 27

Zeke,

Well, the Fitzpatricks are interested in the house. The kid likes the pool, and it sounds like they'll make an offer. No way are they getting it, though.

Here's what happened:

I'm sitting at the kitchen table thinking about doing some of the work I have piled around me and staring at a blank screen. Out of the corner of my eye, I see these three massive, pink faces peeking around the corner, squinting through the sliding glass door. Beyond them, standing by the pool and waving her hands in the air as she talks, is a blonde woman in a navy business suit. Her rouge glows, and I can tell she's talking loud, even though I can't hear her. When I look back toward the bloated, pink faces, they've turned from me without so much as a nod and are walking toward the pool, toward the yammering blonde woman.

I run my hand through my greasy hair and loop some loose strands back over my ears to keep it out of my eyes. Then I hitch up my Levi's, which have been riding low on my hips lately from my inconsistent diet, and go to the back door and lean out.

"You folks want to come in?" I yell. All four of them turn and glance at me, then the three adults turn to one another and confer quietly. The fat kid just keeps staring at me. "Do you want to see the inside?" I say. He just glares, and the others don't even look in my direction. "Suit yourselves," I say and go back in and pop open a Miller Lite. Pretty soon they ring the front doorbell, and I'm thinking to myself, what the hell—why would they come all the way back around to the front? I open the door, and they all stand there for a second, for just a small, awkward pause that should have been filled with some kind of greeting, until the blonde and rouge lady says, "Is Mr. Gretsch in?"

"That's me."

"Oh," she says, her cheeks turning redder, "I thought maybe you were a caretaker. I didn't realize you were the owner."

"Right now, I'm both."

"I was led to believe the house was unoccupied—that immediate possession was available," she says.

"I'm not really living here—just sort of keeping an eye on things. I could be out in a couple of hours."

Meanwhile, the Fitzpatricks have squeezed past us without a word and are poking around out in the living room. They are like Mrs. Waisbloom described them, only bigger. They seem to fill the empty rooms with round, flailing arms and wide hips. If I had antiques or glass collectibles in the house, I'd fear for them.

Mr. Fitzpatrick's feet flop as he walks, and it occurs to me that it's surprising he's the CEO of anything, even the floundering Wire and Cable, given the societal bias against fat and slovenly people. He lumbers up to me and says, "So you're the owner." He eyes me up and down, my bare feet and sagging jeans, the hair and beard.

I play along and try to be friendly. I explain to them that I live in Kansas City, that Mom and Dad were killed in an accident, and, since you died before them, that left me as the only owner. Then the pimply fat boy speaks up.

"You aren't related to Zeke Gretsch are you—that guy that used to play guitar for The Atchison Depot?"

"Yeah, he was my brother."

"No shit? I heard all about him getting killed! It was on MTV and in *Rolling Stone* and all kinds of shit. He was on drugs or something wasn't he?"

I tell him that that's a matter of legal dispute right now—that what killed you was your Jeep rolling over on top of you.

"Well, they all say he was fucked up—pumped full of something." He smiles and sort of sneers at me, challenging me to challenge MTV.

"Knock if off, Jimmy," the old man says. The wife is in the kitchen now with the realtor. The kid just laughs at both of us and starts up the steps to the bedrooms. He stops halfway up and comes back down, his doughy belly swaying over his belt. He comes right up to me and he says, "Hey, this fucking place isn't haunted is it?"

"I beg your pardon?"

"You know, your brother and parents biting the big one. It's their house and all. You don't have ghosts running around here, do you?"

I don't know what to say. The kid has no shame.

"Jimmy, that's enough," the old man says. "Excuse my son. He has what's called inappropriate behavior sometimes."

"Right," I say.

"Excuse what?" the kid says. "Excuse me for not wanting to live in a goddamned spook-infested mansion! He's got to tell us, doesn't he?" He is yelling at the old man now. "He's got to tell us if he knows there are spooks still floating around in here!" The old man's face has turned crimson now.

"Shut up!" the old man says through his teeth. I can feel my face turning red-hot. I want to run up to the fat boy and pop the top of his head off, like a giant zit, and squirt his pus-for-brains onto the ceiling. Instead, I say as calmly as I can that, as far as I know, the place is not haunted.

Just then, the wife and the realtor come back in from the kitchen. Mrs. Waisbloom was right about the wife, too. She seems to fill the hallway, and the breeze she leaves in her wake is spiked with Jim Beam. I can smell it even through the beer on my breath. She's saying something to the realtor about the black and white tiles in the kitchen.

"Those will have to go," she says. "They make me dizzy to look at them."

The realtor says to Mrs. Fitzpatrick, "Getting rid of the tiles is a good idea, dear. What would you put down instead?" They are walking conspiratorily to the den, and I hear one of them say something about indoor-outdoor carpet.

I yell after them. "Hey! Those tiles are great when you get them all shined up and slick. You can slide all the way from here through the kitchen on fresh white socks." The old man looks at me like I'm an idiot. The kid is still staring up the steps, not certain whether he wants to try the upstairs alone. At this point, I'm really starting to get pissed off at these guys, Zeke. In fact, I can taste mad coming up in my throat, way back in my nostrils, so I go to the kitchen to wash it back down. I just sit there sipping my beer until they all congregate in the front hall again. The adults talk quietly, and the kid stares off into space.

"They might be interested," the rouge and lipstick realtor says, trying to be sly. She has pink teeth when she smiles.

I smile back at all of them and want to say, "Well, I'm not. I don't think I can sell to you folks. Nothing personal. I just don't like you." Instead, I say, "Well, fine. You can call my realtor if you have an offer." When I usher them out the door, they don't even thank me for my time. They all seem to flop and slap together like sweaty slabs of meat as they walk down the sidewalk.

Pretty soon my realtor, Mrs. Sisson, calls and tells me she heard from the Fitzpatricks' agent. Mrs. Sisson is a pleasant enough person. She says she thinks we can work something out. She says the Fitzpatricks like the house, and the kid likes the pool and is badgering them to go for it. They want to take one more walk-through and offer me a contract. I hesitate, then I smile to myself a little and say OK. I tell her to see if they can come back on Thursday.

More later, Bro. I have some things to do.

Love,
John

July 28

Zeke,

How you doing, Slick? I've had a big day today, and I'm just about bushed. I'll fill you in before I hit the hay, though.

Bright and early this morning, I had Gary Parker and some of his men from the fire department come over with a truck and pump out the pool. While they were doing that, I went down to Dad's tractor place and had Bobby Cates help me load a backhoe onto a trailer and haul it over to the house. Remember Bobby? He's been there for years. Wears a hearing aid. Anyway, then I borrowed one of the old dump trucks from the tractor lot and went to the north end and picked up a big load of fill dirt. Have you got the picture yet?

Bobby and I had to take down a section of the fence between the Kurzbaums' yard and ours to get the truck and the backhoe in, and Mr. Kurzbaum stood there the whole time, shaking his head saying, "Johnny, Johnny, are you sure you know what you're doing?"

"Believe me, Ira," I said. "This will be best for all of us." Pretty soon, Mrs. Kurzbaum started sending over glasses of iced tea for me and Bobby. She said the backhoe looked like a big yellow dinosaur with stiff joints.

To make a long story short (because I'm tired), we filled the damn thing in. I never used the pool that much anyway. But you'll like this part. For a finishing touch, I got another half-load of dirt and over-filled the hole, so it looks like a mound—like a huge, fresh grave. It was almost dark by the time I got home from taking the equipment back, but I found some two-by-fours out in the garage and hammered them together into three crosses and planted them at the far end of the mound. Then I wove a big wreath out of some of the old man's rose bushes (I cut the hell out of my hands) and placed it near the markers. The Kurzbaums will go nuts when they see it, but I won't leave it for long. Just long enough.

But this is the best thing. I'm smiling to myself about it right now. Remember that "No Diving" sign Dad had by the pool? He was always so liability conscious. Well, I got some paint and a stencil and added to the bottom of it. Now it says "No Diving—Beware of Ghosts." The fat kid will flip. I'll let you know what happens.

Gotta go for now and catch some proper Z's.

Love,
John

July 30

Dear Zeke,

Just a quick communique here to let you know that the earth moving project worked. It was like this: The Fitzpatricks take one look at the backyard and they seem to inflate right there on the spot. They look like three big red balloons ready to pop. They spread out and approach the mound from several different angles, just staring and turning redder and redder. Then their realtor gets in on the color-changing act, and all four of them are flaming and the old man starts sputtering. The fat kid is pumping his fists and saying, "The son of a bitch, Dad. The son of a bitch!"

They all come lumbering and mumbling into the kitchen where I'm standing, and the old man says, "Now just a minute, young man. You signed a realtor's contract, and we were ready to make a very reasonable offer."

"I'll pay the realtor's fee if I have to," I say, "but no sale." I walk to the door and slide it back open for them. They all rumble down onto the patio, the realtor apologizing for the scene, the old man raving about getting a lawyer, and the kid saying over and over, "The son of a bitch, Dad! Can he do it? The son of a bitch!" The wife is trailing along behind, saying "Why does this sort of thing always happen to us? Why?"

Mrs. Sisson called a little later and said she heard all about it from the rouge lady. She said the old man is still talking about getting a lawyer, but I told her not to worry. As far as I know, I don't have to have a pool in my yard if I don't want one. You might notice, I've started referring to this place as "my house" or "my yard." I'm starting to feel anchored here again—weighed down by something. I don't know. For now, though, I'm just going to put on a little Van Morrison, have a cool beer, and think about it. I'm feeling pretty good right now. You might not hear from me for a while.

Love,
John

September 1

An Epistle from John

 Grace be to you, and peace, inhabitants of the other world. Especially you, Zeke. Much has happened since I last wrote.

 First, the Fitzpatricks went away without a fight. They found a house out in Stonecrest. They belong there. Mostly, though, I have come to understand why I couldn't do my work. I couldn't do my work because I didn't want to do my work. Simple.

 For ten years I've been turning mental gymnastics with slicked-back would-be litigators and churning out these multi-footnoted articles that nobody reads—and for what reason? That's the part I've been having trouble with. That's why I've been going over and over things in my head, and turning my open knife over and over in my hand. Why do we do what we do? I guess I just craved a little respectability to offset my eccentricities—my weirdness that I know was always an embarrassment to Dad. "My son?" I thought he could explain to his friends, "Well, you know, he's a professor. They're like that."

 I just never had a retort for those back-slapping, cigar-smoking buddies of his, like the one who asked the old man, when I was eighteen or nineteen, if I was his son or his daughter. I swear, there was malice in the guy's tone. After he left the showroom, Dad said to me, "Never mind him. The guy's a complete asshole." That was the first time Dad ever told me anything like that about the men he knew, but I could tell he was embarrassed. To be a law professor, though! The beard to hide blemished cheeks, the long hair to fit the beard and the quirky personality. Who could argue with such a combination? Certainly not Dad. He would be proud! It was my retort—a way out of some sort of shame from not being the kind of man I think he expected, a way of winning an argument that was never really voiced.

Then, there was little brother Zeke. Not little anymore after all those years. And handsome, and talented. And famous, in a St. Joseph sort of way—the way Jesse James was famous—feared and loved by generations in flux. You were the rock 'n' roll star who lived too fast for the folks back home, even though they still wanted to say they knew you. You were the master of something unique—your music. A gold nameplate—"Associate Professor of Law"—was my consolation prize for your picture in *People* magazine with the beautiful blonde wife in tow. From the pictures, you couldn't even tell that you were from St. Joe and she was from Wathena, Kansas. Both of you were from over the rainbow. And you couldn't cherish all of that enough to preserve it. I just can't understand that right now. What is it that we want that we don't have?

And Mom? Just wanting to make everybody happy. Happy happy happy. She was always so busy with that, she forgot about herself. So I guess if the law professor or the semifamous musician gave her some momentary glory in which to bask, if we sparked some flame of admiration from that woman, then that was another reason for doing what we did. It was our payback, I guess. Just trying to make her a little happy. Happy? Happy? I don't know—maybe you were just in it for the money. But I could see it in their eyes when you came into the room after being far away. God, how you pleased them—and how they died when you died.

Anyway, I've thought about this long and hard, and there just aren't enough reasons now to keep doing what I'm doing. So I quit. Maybe it was a little overdramatic, but that's just the kind of guy I am. Do you remember *Magister Ludi?* I remember you had that and some of Hesse's other stuff lying around the room at one time. Maybe you never read it, but if you did, you might remember this part. What I did was, I sent a circular letter to the dean and the other professors—like the circular letter the master of the glass bead game sent to the board of educators at Castalia when he quit the school there.

I wrote to the dean about how we were sitting at the top of our Castalian edifice, while somewhere down below us, something was burning. I told him how I thought we had taken our place in the university community for granted for too long, and how someday, if we continued to crank out class after class of lawyers (competent or not), our country would decide that we're luxuries it can no longer afford. As the Magister Ludi feared for the players of the glass bead game, I said that I feared we had already become regarded as parasites, tricksters, and enemies. So I quit.

There's nothing new in all this, and I'm not sure what kind of response I expected. The dean and I were never what you could call really close buddies. I got a note back within a few days on university letterhead that just said, "Resignation accepted. Will be in touch regarding your contract. Best personal regards, Dean Axel Attlington."

So to hell with them!

Here's what I've decided to try. Bobby Cates and I are going into the backhoe business. You know? Digging trenches, putting in septic fields, doing highway work. That sort of thing. It feels good to me right now to dig things up—to go below the surface with this big yellow dinosaur with stiff joints, then cover things back over again. Rake it and smooth it, plant grass. It's like creating a new spot on this old earth—like healing a scar. Maybe that's how farmers feel—like they're making a part of the land new again with each plowing and planting. Uncovering, then covering.

I'm also lined up to help with legal aid here in St. Joe. The director is an old classmate of mine, and a couple of the young attorneys are former students. Too weird, huh? It's not much pay, but I don't need much. In fact, I don't need any. I've decided to stay in the house. I moved a couple more pieces of furniture in the other day. So the only housing expense I have will be the upkeep. And the interest alone from the insurance policies and the estate will give me plenty to live on.

Ira Kurzbaum is relieved that I'm staying. He says that even if I'm a strange boy, at least I'm a lovable strange boy. He's so funny. The other day, he's over here talking to me as I'm fixing the fence where we brought the backhoe in, and he says, "Johnny, you know, I've been thinking. If you could cut just a little of the hair—maybe get rid of the ponytail so you don't look like Trigger for crying out loud—I think maybe my niece from Kansas City would be very interested in meeting you. Such a sweet girl—and an artist, too! She does greeting card pictures for Hallmark." I thanked him for the possibility of the introduction and told him that I might cut my hair a little. That made him perfectly happy, and Mrs. Kurzbaum brought me some more iced tea.

Then yesterday I heard from Lisa. She called to see how I was doing and she said she was doing fine. She sounded great, Zeke. She's selling real estate in LA. Can you believe it? Says she wants nothing to do with the music scene anymore. I told her about the Fitzpatricks and the pool and the huge grave, and she laughed until she couldn't catch her breath and called me weird and macabre (again, rhyming with sabre). I don't know if we'll keep in touch, but at least I think we ended on a friendly note.

I don't know if you could tell, but I've been treading pretty close to the edge over the past few months. Sometimes I've been drinking a little too much, and I've been doing this thing with my knife. I'm feeling much better about things now, though. And I'm glad I kept in touch with you about it. It's been a bitch, being left behind. By the way, you might not hear from me for a while again. I'll be busy with these new jobs and all, and pretty soon I'll be putting this old yard to bed for the winter. Oh, and I think I'll put a garden in next spring—in the pool full of dirt. Maybe some veggies, maybe some flowers—some more roses. Right now, though, it's sunrise, and I think I'll take my cup of coffee and walk around outside for a while. The yard is just starting to fill with those first golden, misty rays of light that filter through the big maples across the fence. The air is cool and heavy with moisture this morning, and the wet grass will cling to my bare feet as I walk. Peace, Brother.

Love always,
John

Singleton

PEOPLE KEEP sending me copies of my uncle's obituary, and I don't know why. I know he died. I was there. I was at the funeral. Do some people collect these things, these little snippets of not quite accurate facts?

Before I went to law school, I was a newspaper reporter, and like every other reporter, I started by doing obituaries. The city editor used to say to me, "John, most folks only get their names in the paper three times—when they're born, when they get married, and when they die—so you have to get the facts and the spelling right. It's important to them." It was always a little unclear to me why it was important to the dead person, but I guess he meant it was important to the survivors. Well, I'm a survivor now, one of the surviving nephews you could read about in my uncle's obituary, and I can see now how the most carefully crafted of these tiny biographies sometimes omits so much it might as well be about someone else's life. For instance, I happen to have a copy of my uncle's obituary right here, and it says that Henry Sheridan, age 79, was the son of Philip and Fanny Sheridan, and that he was preceded in death by his parents; by his wife, Naomi; by his brother, John; and by his sister, Maude. Then it says he is survived by several nieces and nephews. That's the part where I come in, but there is a lot more to it than that.

Uncle Henry, who was taller than anyone else in the family, was the oldest of the three children and, according to most accounts, was my grandmother's favorite. My mother, who has never really liked Henry much I guess, has said again and again how much that old woman, meaning my grandmother, doted on Henry and pushed him and encouraged him in the things he did in life, while my father and Aunt Maude were left to fend for themselves. No matter what trouble he caused, no matter how he failed her or the rest of the family, my grandmother always sided with Henry, was always supportive of him, and expected nothing in return. At least that's the way my mother saw it. "Your father, on the other hand," she would say, "stayed right here and cared for your grandmother until her dying day, but it was never good enough. It was always Henry this or Henry that."

I suppose it is true that Henry lorded it over the family, as oldest sons often do, and that might be why I have sometimes felt a certain affinity toward him. I am an oldest son and know something about the unjustified, inexplicable, yet very real feeling that, because I'm the oldest, the family and the world revolve around me. Maybe it has something to do with the vestiges of primogeniture, but it manifests itself in little bursts of selfishness that mothers, it seems, are all too willing to accommodate.

My father, John, and his sister, Maude, were born when Henry was five years old. To hear folks tell it, Grandmother had a terrible time with the birthing of the twins, and they almost lost her and the babies. Beyond that, nobody ever talked much about what it was like to have two new babies around the house. Even when my grandfather was still alive, the most he had to say about the whole event was, "Oh, yes. That was quite a thing in those days, quite a thing." Even though John and Maude obviously weren't identical twins, they did favor one another in looks, which was all right for my father but didn't do my aunt Maude any good. She was a long time getting a husband, and when she did, he was a backward, painfully shy bookkeeper for a furniture business there in Westgate, Missouri, where my father was born and where most of this takes place. Oliver, Maude's husband, had a liver ailment of some kind that killed him by the time he was forty, but not before he and Maude managed to have two children, my cousins, Dory and Kay, who were several years younger than my sister, Jean, and myself. My father stayed in Westgate, too, and married my mother and took over my grandfather's small tool and die business after the old man passed on. So John and Maude never were too far away from Grandmother and her big old Victorian house up on Hall Street. Henry, on the other hand, got work with the railroad when he was eighteen years old and never came back except to visit and, years later, to die.

The thing to know about Uncle Henry is he had money, lots of money. He had the kind of money that he had to put in trusts and limited partnerships and such to keep it away from the IRS. He married into it when he married Naomi, his second wife, who was from one of the big meat-packing families in Kansas City. The other thing to know about Henry is, because he hadn't always had money, he was cheap when it came to certain things, which is where I come in again later.

Henry met Naomi when he was a brakeman on the old St. Joe to Hannibal run for the Missouri-Pacific. She was on her way to Chicago, and by the time they reached Hannibal, she had agreed to see him when she came back to Kansas City.

"He was a charmer in those days," Aunt Naomi used to say. "And handsome. He could talk a girl into just about anything." And to hear my mother and father talk about it, he was reckless with such charms, too. Apparently Grandmother had to "make arrangements" to get Henry out of trouble with several girls by the time he left home at age eighteen. It's hard to say what kind of destruction he left in his wake after that, although he did leave his first wife to marry Naomi. I don't know much about the first wife, except my mother referred to her as "that sweet child from Hannibal." I know they were childless, as were Henry and Naomi.

For some reason, when Henry and Naomi came to visit, they stayed with us rather than with my grandmother, who had the big Victorian house all to herself, and Aunt Naomi served as the entertainment committee for the children. She was a compact woman, firm and tight like a knotted rope, and had the calves of a ballet dancer, like clenched fists at the back of her legs that gave her an extra bounce as she walked. She had been a ballerina when she was young, and her parents had given her voice lessons—training for the opera, as if the meat-packing money could buy culture for Kansas City. So when Henry and Naomi came to town, the neighborhood kids and my cousins would join us in our garage for Naomi to direct us in a makeshift song-and-dance production, as if we were in a Mickey Rooney movie. They usually came twice a year, Christmas and July, all except the year my uncle joined the army toward the end of World War II and spent the duration at Fort Dix, New Jersey. My mother said that was the craziest stunt he ever pulled, joining the army at age thirty-five, but my grandmother defended him, saying that Henry was just patriotic, just like his father Philip, and that Philip would have done the same thing if he were alive. My father just laughed when he heard that, and said, "For crying out loud, if Dad were alive he'd rather be taken over by the Germans than go to New Jersey."

When Henry got out of the army, that was another thing he lorded it over my father about and would ride him to the point where sometimes I thought my mother would burst or do some violence to Henry with a small kitchen appliance. If Henry was going to correct my father about the way he was doing something, which he did daily, he often would start with "Now, if you had been in the service like I was, you'd know that . . ."—and then go on to tell Dad at length how it should be done. My father would just smile slightly to himself and then go about doing it the way he was doing it, as if he could just tune Henry out with the defective hearing that he had had since birth and that had kept him out of the service.

Uncle Henry also was big on telling us how things were done on the railroad. He seemed to have three basic standards for measuring quality in all things, the army, the railroad, and Cadillac, the only car I ever remember seeing him drive. There might have been others, but from 1953, when I was sixteen and was becoming aware of such things, until the day Henry died, he owned a Cadillac that was never more than two or three years old. He doted on those cars as if they were his children.

When Henry and Naomi visited us in July, they were usually on their way to somewhere else, on one of their many cross-country Cadillac tours. They went to Mexico one year, to Alaska another year. They even went to Europe one year, but left the Cadillac at home. Once, I remember my mother saying to Grandmother that maybe she and Dad would like to go with Naomi and Henry on one of their driving trips across country sometime, and my Grandmother said, "Oh, I don't think that would be a good idea, dear. I don't think you and John travel in the same social circles as Henry and Naomi. John might be uncomfortable, not having as much money and all." My mother bit back saying anything, but she turned red, and I remember her being cold toward Grandmother for weeks after that.

Things were pretty much the same between Henry and Maude, I guess, except Henry seemed to have even less to do with her and her sickly husband. I do remember though that he came to Uncle Oliver's funeral and sat with the family and cried and moaned and carried on as if he'd lost his best friend, and he said over and over again to Aunt Maude that he'd see to it that my cousins never wanted for anything. I don't know if he ever helped them out that much, but I do know that my cousins had to wear a lot of my sister's clothes when she was through with them. Dory and Kay were always four or five years out of style.

Like I said, Henry was cheap when it came to some things. That's how he ended up in the Veterans Administration hospital in Westgate when he came down sick after Naomi died. And that's how I got to know Uncle Henry better and how I got to know just how wrong his seemingly innocent obituary is.

Aunt Naomi dropped dead on one of the exit ramps at a Kansas City Chiefs football game two years ago. Uncle Henry always had season tickets. On that chilly Sunday evening, though, Aunt Naomi's old dancer's heart gave out on her and, in a way, so did Henry's. He was never the same after that, his memory coming and going at random and his blood pressure soaring like the temperature in a pottery kiln.

Most everyone was gone by then, Grandmother years ago, my father and Aunt Maude just a couple of years before Naomi. So one day six months ago, Henry called me at my office and said he was coming to Westgate to check into the VA hospital—that his doctor had recommended hospitalization, but he wasn't going to pay for a fancy private hospital when he could get care for free because he was a veteran.

"But Henry, you've got all the money you need," I said. "You might get better care at a private hospital there in Kansas City."

"Don't be silly," he said. "The army doesn't do things halfway. VA hospitals are probably the best. Besides, it's free."

At the VA hospital, they controlled his blood pressure with medication, and for his memory loss and periods of confusion, they put him in the psychiatric ward with hollowed-out, shell-shocked old World War II vets and wild-eyed bearded Vietnam basket cases. He became even more confused and asked me if I thought he was crazy.

I spoke to one of the young doctors who seemed to be in charge, a balding, nervous young man whose bony fingers constantly tugged and twisted at the knot of his tie. "We think these fits of confusion and memory loss may be signs of depression," he said. "So, that's how we're treating him—for depression."

"I thought they were signs of old age," I said.

Henry suffered mostly from short-term memory loss. Sometimes he wouldn't remember my name when I came to visit, and he wouldn't remember what he had for breakfast an hour earlier, or if he had even had breakfast. Yet, as if to compensate, his failing mind would conjure up such vivid images of the past that he would blurt things out about them at random. Once in a while, the images would come together in such a pattern that Henry would be able to tell me a story about a particular event or person in his past, and tell it with such detail it was as if it had taken place just yesterday.

On one of my visits, Henry sat in a rocking chair near the window and stared out over the hospital lawn toward an abundantly lush cornfield across the way. Suddenly, he turned to me and said, "Johnny, when I'm gone, you're going to have to do something for me. Will you do it?"

"I don't know," I said. "What's it about?"

"It's about the only other woman I ever truly loved besides Naomi," he said. He motioned for me to slide my chair over closer to his, and he leaned in toward me, speaking softly and conspiratorily. "It was years ago, when I was just a pup, before I met your aunt. Even before I was married the first time. Your mama probably told you that I was a little wild in those days, and I guess I was. But Anna, her name was Anna Klineczek, she stopped me in my tracks." If there was something wrong with his memory, it wasn't apparent this day, as his eyes glazed at the remembrance and he launched into two accounts, punctuated with tears and smiles, that changed forever the way I thought about Uncle Henry. The first story was about Anna.

Anna Klineczek, Uncle Henry said, was the most fascinating woman he ever loved or met, not because of classic beauty or grace, of which she lacked full measures, but because she remained forever mysterious. He said Anna must have been on the shady side of thirty years old when he met her, and he was only twenty-two and had just started his job on the run between St. Joe and Hannibal. Through luck and an accident that injured a couple of men who were his seniors, Henry had become one of the youngest brakemen on the Missouri-Pacific. Henry was friends with the conductor, who was like the captain of a ship, and the conductor allowed Henry to stroll the passenger cars and chat with the young girls, impressing them with the crisp bill of his cap and his bright red bandanna. He was lucky indeed to have such a job. It was 1932 and the Depression had hit hard. So what happened between Henry and the mysterious and married Mrs. Klineczek happened at great risk. It began in an empty compartment on a Pullman car on one of Mrs. Klineczek's weekly trips from Brookfield to Chillicothe.

Henry had seen Anna before, had admired her tallness and her stride, the way she swung her arms and clicked her heels aggressively, almost like a man. She had dark, crinkly crisp hair that she curled under slightly at her shoulders, and her arms and face were brown, a farm wife tan. Uncle Henry said she wasn't a classic beauty but had a pleasant face, one that let its best features shine through. She had a slight bump on her nose that was not altogether unpleasant, and full lips, parted and moist, as if she could almost taste something. But her best feature, he said, was her eyes. She had beautiful, catlike brown eyes that could penetrate and attract, could pull you right into them and make you forget there was a job or a farm or anything else.

"That's how it was the first time," Henry said. "I was just standing talking to her at the door of the compartment, I don't even know what about, and her eyes just pulled me to her. She kept them open the whole time, as if she couldn't see enough. We were mostly just pulled-out shirts and hiked-up dresses, but those chocolate, almond eyes were wide open and darting over everything, like she had to take it in all at once and didn't want to miss a single feature of it." After that, Henry and Anna went on disheveling and reassembling in the Pullman car on a weekly basis for almost a year while she traveled from Brookfield to Chillicothe to see her ailing mother. Somehow, the Pinkertons never caught Henry.

Anna's husband was Rexford Klineczek, whose grand and regal-sounding name apparently was an irony. He was a bean farmer who stayed pretty much to the farm, except for an occasional trip as far west as Cameron during turkey and deer hunting season.

"He's pure Brookfield," Anna told Henry. "He has his hunting, but beyond that, he's pure Brookfield."

Henry said it was hard to get her to talk at first, like trying to take her wisdom teeth, but gradually she revealed bits and pieces of her life, like precious pebbles fetched up from a mine. Rexford was nearly twenty years her senior, and they were childless during the ten years of their marriage. It was a failure that had become a sore point in their lives, a failure to produce that, on the farm, had economic as well as emotional consequences. Rexford became withdrawn, even more taciturn than ever, and Anna spent long hours contemplating a change, grappling with the hunger that kept her lips moist and parted, as if she were about to speak, as if she were prepared to taste anything that was offered to her. That is when her mother came down sick and she started making her sojourns home, and that is when she met the young, handsome railroad man who was my uncle.

Henry said he was wild for her, and sometimes she was wild, too, like a lioness, and would present herself to him rearward, pressing hard back against him, bracing herself on the arms of a seat, pushing toward him with those strong, brown arms. Even during those times, he said, she kept her eyes open, her teeth touching her bottom lip, and watched their reflections in the window glass as dusk settled in behind the dark green waves of corn and beans that rolled before them. It was during one of those times that she became pregnant.

"Somehow I knew it as soon as it happened," Anna told

Henry. "Don't ask me how, but there was just something, and all of a sudden I knew it, just as surely as I knew there were beans in front of me and you at the back of me."

After he calmed himself to it all, Henry said, "What will you tell your husband?"

"Nothing," she said. "I can't tell him nothing. After ten years of drought, he'll know this crop I'll be harvesting isn't his. I'll tell him nothing."

"You'll leave him, then," Henry said, "and we'll marry." She just smiled slightly and looked at him as if he were a child who got the wrong answer in school.

"That's when I made my mistake," Henry told me. "I told Mother about us. Without giving all the details, I told her enough about the situation so she would know why I needed the money I was asking for, why I planned to move to Kansas City permanently, to be absorbed into the city." Henry's sunken, gray eyes took on a hard glint, and his mottled, paperlike face seemed to darken even as he thought about it.

"I don't know how Mother found her," he said, "or how she contacted her or what was said. But the next time I saw Anna, the only things I could get out of her were sobs and nonsense talk about how she could take care of everything herself and I shouldn't worry about her anymore. She just sat all in a pile in the seat, arms and legs crossed, and stared out the window."

Uncle Henry said he never saw her again after that. He went to Brookfield and Chillicothe and asked around, saying it was railroad business—something about a package she had reported missing from the train. He found out soon enough that she had just disappeared, just packed a suitcase one day as if she were going on her weekly trip and never came back. Nobody, not even her husband, had heard from her, and when her mother died inside of a year after her leaving, she didn't even come to Chillicothe to the funeral.

"I just moped around for a while after that," Henry said. "It was one of those times when there was real poison between Mother and me, and I just let it build up until we weren't hardly speaking. Then I met my first wife, Elsie, and married her to spite Mother more than anything else, I guess. Elsie was just a simple thing, and her people in Hannibal didn't have much of a reputation to speak of. Mother was fit to be tied."

A faint smile pulled at the corners of Henry's mouth and water began to well up in his yellow, dry eyes. "Elsie was a sweet and simple thing. I'm sorry I ever did that to her, but Mother—that grandmother of yours—she made me crazy more than once in my life."

"I always thought you were her favorite," I said. "It sounds like maybe she was just trying to help in her own way."

Henry paused, a confused expression, a blankness, settling in around his eyes and mouth, as if he were trying to remember something, and he said, "She was good at appearances and expected nothing less of her children." He shifted in his chair, and color rose up in his cheeks, pronounced veins forming purple ridges on his neck and forehead. "I was her favorite because that's what was expected, that's what was usual."

"Is that why you stayed away so much?" I said. "You were staying away from her?"

"She and I were always apart, even when we were together," he said. "At least ever since the babies were born."

"You mean Dad and Maude?" I said. "You mean all these years you let a little sibling rivalry, a little jealousy, sour you on all those good people?"

Henry seemed surprised by my impatient tone. Then he smiled again, a sad, regretful smile, his lower lip quivering, and shook his head back and forth, whispering, "No, no, no." He leaned forward again, his thin hands clasped in front of him, and said, "Johnny, I'm going to tell you something, not because I want you to think any less of anybody, but just so you know the way things were. Then, like I said, I'd like you to do something for me." He hacked and rattled with a dry, dry cough, then started in on an incredible tale about Grandmother and the birth of the triplets. Triplets!

"There were three of them, Johnny," he said. "Nobody ever talked about the third one after any of this, and John, your father, and Maude, they never knew any of it. Folks who knew were just mum. They pretended like I didn't know, but Mother knew that I knew. It was a home birth, which is why it's amazing any of them survived, but the littlest one—he never made it past the first few hours. Old Doc Walker was there, and a midwife, but they never said anything either, and the birth certificates were made out for twins."

I sat stunned, unblinking, but thought to ask how he knew all of this.

"I had ears," he said. "I had eyes. I was only five, but I was no fool, and I wasn't always asleep when the grown-ups thought I was."

"What happened to the third one?" I said. "What was wrong?"

"I don't know that for sure," Henry said. "I've suspected there was something wrong with it so that everybody just sort of agreed to let him go without really talking about it out loud. Especially after what happened later." Tears began to shine at the corners of his eyes, the way they do in old people sometimes when they talk about long ago things.

"Mother wasn't really like this at all before the babies were born," he said. "I mean, she was the sweetest thing. Not a care in the world except to make me happy. Then, after the babies, for a long time after, nobody could go near her. She would howl like an animal, all latched up inside her room, not caring for the live babies at all. And when she did come out, she would glide through the house in her nightgown, her hair all wild and undone, and hover in the corners of the rooms like a ghost. Dad was like a ghost then, too. He would disappear completely during the day, and at night, he came and went from her room, trying to tend to her. I guess she had what you would call that postpartum depression, the baby blues, but she had it to the point of madness—that's what folks called it in those days. They would say, 'She's got the madness from those children.'"

Henry said that gradually she began taking the babies back from the wet nurse, but there were still late-night, whispered discussions about John, the boy baby who survived but who was failing to thrive. There was something about blindness and deafness—that he might never walk. His mother would carry the limp child in one arm, the flailing, howling Maude in the other, and weep throughout the house. And Henry, the singleton, was forgotten for a time.

"I had to spy on her—had to follow her around just to be close to her at all," he said. "When I tried to talk to her, she just stared through me or gazed beyond me, like she was fixed on something hanging on the blank wall behind me." Henry himself stared for a moment, another lapse that brought tears, and he rubbed nervously at the front of his blue-striped robe with his purple-spotted hands.

"Then one day I was looking for her, trying to follow her. I heard water running in the tub upstairs and I heard Maude howling as usual. Mother was always very fussy about knocking, and I knew just as I was doing it that I shouldn't have been opening the bathroom door, but something made me do it anyway." Henry began to rock back and forth, patting clenched fists on his thin knees, tears streaking his dry cheeks now.

"That's when things changed, Johnny," he said, his voice scratchy and shaking. He spoke slowly now, choosing his words carefully. "Just in those few seconds at that six-inch gap in the door, I saw the weakness in Mother—something she loved and hated me for from then on. She never said a word about it, and neither did I. We didn't have to. We both knew that tub was too full—way too full. We knew from the way our eyes met that we understood one another. My eyes moved from the baby boy in her arms to the tub and back again, and I knew that I had seen her at her worst, at her weakest, all appearances stripped away. And she knew that I would try to separate myself from it all, lock it all away, stay alone with it and never really be a part of them."

"She was going to drown Dad?" I said, my throat constricting.

Henry nodded slowly and said, "But don't think her evil for it, Johnny. It was the madness. I know it was. That and the notion that maybe the live baby boy wasn't much better off than the dead one—being all limp and the doctor talking about blindness and lameness."

"Well, what happened then?" I said.

"Nothing," he said. "She just flustered around and asked that I excuse myself, like maybe I had walked in on her while she was climbing out of her underthings. Then she drained some of the water and went about the business of bathing the babies. I heard her sobbing the whole time, though."

"I mean with Dad," I said. "What happened?"

"He grew out of it," said Henry. "I guess he was just weak for a while and got a slow start from being born one of three. He didn't start to walk until he was two years old, but he came around eventually. He did have that bad hearing, though."

We sat silently for a time, Henry twisting the edge of his robe with gnarled fingers. That's when I noticed how much his hands reminded me of Grandmother's—the long, delicately tapered fingers, all knotted now into arthritic bunches.

"Anyway, Johnny," he said finally, "that's what I wanted you to know. That's why we all seemed the way we did, I think. Separate, not connected. I know what your mother thought about us—that we were just plain selfish and stuck-up compared to your father. She might have been partly right, I guess, but there was just more to it than that. John was a good man, but there was always more to it. Maybe jealousy that he and Maude were so innocent about it all. Maybe resentment that Mother and I came apart some because of them, and resentment that Mother had to work so hard at making it appear that it wasn't so. I don't know. You just get into a pattern with folks, and it's hard to break out."

Henry stared out the window, his dry face drained of its color. After a few moments of letting it all sink in, I said, "If it was real—everything you saw and heard—how could entire lifetimes pass without folks knowing, without somebody saying something?"

"You of all people should know, Johnny," he said. "You're a lawyer. Aren't there times when a few folks who know something agree, without agreeing out loud, that something never happened—that no questions will be asked?" I had to admit there were such times, but still found it difficult to picture Grandmother in such a state of weakness and despair and capable of making such wrong decisions.

Henry gave a sigh and a beatific smile, as if relieved of a great weight, and said, "There now, I've told the two things I wanted you—wanted somebody—to know. About Anna and about Mother—and about some truth." He leaned forward again, as if to draw me in close. "Now, this is what I wanted you to do for me, Johnny. When Anna ran off all those years ago, I'm sure she had the baby. She wouldn't have done anything else. I've tried off and on over the years to track her down, but it was hard to do in secret. I thought you might know of a way. Aren't there folks who do that—search for missing heirs?" I told him there were investigators who did such things, if he was sure he wanted to search.

"This Anna might not be alive, Henry," I said. "She was older than you, remember?"

"I know," he said. "I know. But what about the child, or what about grandchildren?"

"You don't want them to know, do you?" I said.

"Absolutely not!" he said. "There would be no point in that. But I thought some money, part of the estate, could be given anonymously if you find them. What about that?" I told him there might be a way to work something like that out—if Anna and her family could be found—if things could be verified.

Henry gave a little huff and said, "I don't care if you're certain or not. Just give it to them if you can trace her. I'm not going to have any use for the money, and you and your sister and Maude's family will get plenty. Will you do it for me, Johnny?" I told him I would think it through and we could talk about it the next Sunday.

That was the last time I saw Henry. You never know what really goes on in a big place like that VA hospital, but the doctors all say that it had nothing to do with the medication they were giving him. They say that two days after my last visit, Henry complained of dizziness and some slight chest pain and some pain in his left arm. He died some time during the night, but nobody knows when exactly.

When I went to the hospital later to pick up some of Henry's personal belongings, a giant of a man came toward me down the hallway. I recognized him as one of the wild-eyed Vietnam vets from the psychiatric ward. His name was Billy Bob and he was huge, with a beard and long hair pulled back in a ponytail. He wore a black T-shirt that said "Harley-Davidson" across his massive chest, and he reminded me of a redneck fiddle player from a country and western band I had seen once. He walked straight toward me, his arms outstretched, his red face pinched into either a smile or a glare, and reached for me. His huge, bear-hug arms enveloped me, and he sobbed over me.

"I'm so sorry about Henry," he wept, his voice smoke-scarred and clogged with phlegm. "He was a good old bastard," he said. "One of the sweetest old gents you'd ever want to meet. I'm just sorry I only got to know him for such a short time."

"I know," I said. "Me too."

Billy Bob laughed then, wiping his cheek with the back of his hand, and said, "That old boy did have some stories, didn't he? Interesting. Interesting. Hard to tell sometimes where truth left off and bullshit began. But he was a sweetheart to me, I'll tell you that."

"I know," I said. "I know what you mean. A life that long, it's hard to verify the facts sometimes." I patted his big arm and thanked him for his thoughts.

What I am doing now is trying to verify some of the facts. I'm a fact checker. I'm a survivor looking for more survivors, starting in Brookfield and expanding out from there. And I wish folks would quit sending me newspaper clippings with Henry's obituary, as if the truth of things were memorialized there. I used to be a reporter, so I know sometimes a story can get all balled up. Mistakes get made. Eventually, corrections appear.

On King Hill

APRIL LEANS back in the rear seat of the 1950 Studebaker smoking Old Gold filters, the kind of cigarettes she and all her girlfriends smoke. She is seventeen and Bobby, sitting next to her, is seventeen, and they both like the way the smoke looks as it curls softly from their lips, from their long, thin fingers. That is why they smoke. They prop their feet on the back of the front seat and take long, deep drags from their cigarettes. April's jeans are tight, but they feel good. They feel like they look good, and she would rather feel a little cramp in the stomach than feel loose and baggy. She knows she looks good in the jeans because her legs are the kind of legs that some boys might say "go on forever," and her rear end and thighs are firm, no bulges. She leans forward to flip her ashes out the window and she rests her chin on the back of the fuzzy front seat.

All of South St. Joseph is spread before them like a dark sea of once rich bottomland flickering with the streetlights and house lights that emerge at dusk below King Hill, where they are parked. Bobby has parked near the edge of the hill, near a row of large limestone boulders that rim the lookout point. The flat landscape beyond the Missouri River, with only a few lights scattered here and there, is like a dim mirror that reflects the true image of the high, clear spring night that has opened above them. But far off to the west, a line of thunderclouds, trimmed in orange, rolls up from the Kansas horizon like a mushrooming mountain range.

They sit silently smoking as more and more lights bloom from the blackness below them. The smoke makes April light-headed, so she opens the window more to let out some of the steam and smoke. Parked behind them, across the parking lot and facing the other direction, is a 1968 Camaro with strains of Van Morrison's "Brown Eyed Girl" seeping from its fogged windows. It is the only other car on the hill tonight. April is still light-headed, so she opens the rear door and climbs onto one of the boulders, hugging her knees with her elbows and cupping the cigarette in her hand. Bobby joins her and they stare into the night.

"The drive-in is starting already," Bobby says.

"Where?" April says. They don't look at each other as they speak.

"Look, down there."

Far below, like a calling card set on edge, the screen at the Cowtown drive-in theater is lit with colorful, moving images. April squints and puts her hand above her eyes, visorlike, as if that will help her to see more clearly far away, in the dark. The images begin to take shape, and she can make out two tiny flesh forms moving rhythmically against one another. April groans, "Ugh! Are they still showing those X-rated movies at that place? I thought they made them quit because of the traffic hazards. You can see it right from the road down there."

"Yeah, they said it was like shouting 'fire' at a crowded

theater," Bobby says. "Did you ever hear anything so stupid? Looks like they're back at it again this year, though." He still does not look at her and is silent for a while, leaning back on the boulder and watching his own smoke stream satisfyingly from his puffed lips. Then he speaks and leans forward to look at her. "I don't understand why you won't let me show you how much I love you. We've been going together for over four months—since the Christmas dance."

"Don't talk to me about love. We don't know what that is. That's not what you're talking about. Besides, I didn't say I wouldn't. I just said not now."

"But you've been saying not now for quite a while." Bobby leans forward more as he speaks, trying to look her full in the face, but she turns from him slightly. She leans back now, stretching her T-shirt over her flat stomach, flattening her braless breasts. She stares straight up into the stars and blows a lazy smoke ring that rises two feet into the restless air before it wavers and breaks up. Her high cheeks are flushed, her lips puffy like his own, and her dark hair flares beneath her as if arranged for some seductive photograph. He knows at that moment that she is absolutely the most beautiful girl (woman? he doesn't know what to call her) that he has ever seen, and certainly the most beautiful he has ever kissed. He has only kissed one other girl—the girl that he dumped as soon as he caught on to hallway rumors that April might go to the Christmas dance with him if he were to ask. He is deranged by the need to kiss April, just to touch her hand, or even just to sit near her in the rear seat of his car. But now he is trying to act like he is becoming impatient and angry, trying to push her to the edge, to see how cold and demanding he can be and still feel safe in the notion that she loves him too, in whatever foal-legged form love can take for eleventh-graders of a serious bent.

Even though he is sure his health would fail if he were to lose her, he says, "Well, maybe we should just break up and date other people if now isn't the right time." He thinks his tone is icy enough to be convincing.

"You know you don't mean that," she says, smiling up at him. She reaches up to him then and kisses him with her mouth open, pressing hard against lips still swollen from the recent bout in the back seat. She holds her cigarette off to one side and entwines her free hand in his long blonde hair as she pulls him toward her. She wants him often, wants to pull his whiplike, almost hairless body to her, with her jeans in a tangle around her ankles, and envelop him. She wants to clutch at him while his long hair falls around her face and brushes along her breasts, her stomach. But then there is the fear, and a kind of nonspecific malaise that overcomes her, that makes her want to break away first. "Not now, Bobby," she whispers, and gently pulls back from his hands at her shirt.

He buries his head in her shoulder. Suddenly he does a push-up off the rock and bounces to his feet beside her. "Fine!" he says. "Just fine. Except now you made me lose my cigarette. It was my last one." April watches him huff and stomp around the boulder as he looks for his cigarette, and she smiles at how easy and unthreatened she feels with this delicate boy, even when he pretends to be angry. It is so unlike the way it was with her father, whose sheer bulk and seething unhappiness made him seem dangerous and terrifying, even though he never harmed her physically. A wash of fear makes her twitch with a chill when she thinks of him and the power he must have had. She has not seen him since she was nine, since her mother died, even though he tried at first to get custody of her and her brother. Now it is hard for her to conjure up images of him except those of the last few months before her mother's death, images of broad movements, loud late-night discussions, and a heavy, grimly set jaw.

She smiles now though at Bobby's antics as he casts about in the dust for his lone, half-smoked cigarette. He is playing the buffoon now, rather than the proud, wounded male.

"I'll tell you what," he says. "I'm sure not going to smoke any of those coffin nails of yours. Those are killers."

April laughs, "Oh, must baby have his little menthol filters?" She leans over and pokes at him. "Besides, I didn't offer you any."

"You'd at least let me bum a cigarette, wouldn't you? You could at least put out that much!" He smiles down at her, trying to look sinister, but his eyebrows raise in such a way that he simply looks surprised. "I've got the car, remember? Put out or get out. Hit the bricks baby!"

"Who's going to make me?" April says as she rolls from the rock and scuttles, almost on all fours, across the pavement and back through the open rear door of the car. Bobby plunges in after her, grunting and laughing, falling on her from behind. He brushes her hair to the side with the back of his hand, lightly kisses her neck, and inhales her hair and its baby shampoo scent. "Watch it," she says, squirming beneath him, "we're going to start something we can't finish if we're not careful."

"No we won't." He suddenly raises himself above her and straddles her legs. "I do have something we can finish, though." He climbs over the seat and bounces down into the front, banging his leg on the steering wheel. "Ouch! Shit!" Then he reaches into the glove compartment and eases out what is left of a fifth of Wild Turkey whiskey.

"Firewater!" April says, gasping in feigned shock.

"Firewater?" says Bobby. "You're into that Indian junk of your grandmother's too much."

"No, really," she says, turning the bottle in her hands to examine the label. "This stuff literally is firewater. I saw Jimmy Kawalski toss a match into a saucer full of this stuff at a party once. It burns like rocket fuel."

"Yeah, I've seen that," Bobby says, following the bottle back over the seat. He plops down beside her. "So, how is old Grandmother Squaw anyway?"

"Don't call her that," April says. "That doesn't sound nice. Besides, I've been reading through some of those old books she has, and I think she could be right—she could have the Indian blood she claims, going way back to the days of Joe Robidoux." It was widely rumored, and by some historians reported as fact, that Joseph Robidoux, the fur-trading founder of St. Joseph, Missouri, had several bastard children by Indian squaws with whom he kept extramarital company, and it is this lineage to which April's eccentric grandmother lays claim.

"Did you really read all those books of hers?" he says.

"Not all, but a lot."

The fact that April reads so much, that she is so intelligent, excites Bobby. She reads everything she can find—poetry, history, novels by Russians Bobby cannot even pronounce—and she is in the National Honor Society. He wonders how she can do that. How can she know so much and still want to be here with him? Not that he is a dunce—he just considers himself more of a plodder, while people like April soar. Their intellectual difference reinforces Bobby's notion that their attraction is of the spirit—of essentials that don't have to make sense—and that notion makes her all the more exciting to him. It's like something that can't be stopped, like the roiling Missouri River below them, or the towering thunderclouds sweeping toward them across the dry Kansas plain. What they have will just go and go until it is spent—until it is spent grandly and desperately. It will not simply dry up. He takes a quick drink from the bottle and gasps as he chokes it down, squeezing out tears from the corners of his eyes. "Want some?" he says, passing April the bottle. She takes a small sip and makes a face. Then she takes a longer drink and coughs as it goes down. She leans back and props her feet on the front seat again.

April waves her hand around in a broad, sweeping motion. "You know, all this—this hill is supposed to be very historical. It was an Indian battleground and all that."

"I remember," Bobby says. "They taught us all about it in grade school." He lifts the bottle gently from April, who sits staring into the accumulating blackness of the approaching storm. The stars have disappeared now in the west, replaced by muted flashes of distant lightning.

"The battleground part is minor, though," April says, her voice lowering almost to a whisper. "I bet they didn't teach you about the human sacrifices."

"What human sacrifices? Where did you hear about that?"

"In some of Grandma's old books," she says and looks straight at him. Her face seems to darken as she speaks. "Imagine this place, long before any white men came here. There's no parking lot here, no rusting water tanks, or broken beer bottles, or old used condoms. There's no traffic moving slowly along Lake Avenue down below. This would be an Iowa camp on top of this hill, because the Iowas had wiped out the Missouri tribe in a big battle here—the one they teach you about in school. To tell the truth, though, it probably wasn't much of a battle. The Missouris already had been almost wiped out by disease—smallpox or something. But this hill was their burial ground, so they had to defend it as best they could when the Iowas attacked. Neither tribe was much of a warrior tribe. Basically, they didn't exert themselves very much. In a word, they were wimps. But the Iowas were less wimpy than the Missouris, I guess. The Iowas called themselves 'dusty noses' and some of the other tribes called them 'the sleepy ones.'"

Bobby laughs. "Hey, maybe they were on drugs."

"Who knows?" April shrugs. "Maybe peyote or something." Bobby looks puzzled, and April knows that he has never heard of peyote before. She lifts the bottle from Bobby's lap and takes another sip. Then she lights another Old Gold and takes a long, deep drag, holding the cigarette elegantly in the V of her first two fingers and pulling it away from her dramatically, as she imagines a teller of stories should.

"Anyway, just imagine being up here then, and we are in the Iowa tribe. It's our camp now and we live here. At night, the only lights we can see will be from our campfires and the stars and the moon. During the day, when we look toward the west, all we can see is the big river winding through the flatland, all lined with cottonwoods and willows, disappearing behind the wooded bluffs to the south. And out there, where the sun goes down, it's not even Kansas yet. It's just gently rolling grassland as far as the eye can see. Sometimes we see a great billow of dust moving across the plain, like an isolated storm. The land seems to undulate as the dust storm appears and disappears at the crests of the grass hills. At the center of the great cloud, there's a dark mass that grows blacker and larger as the storm nears the river. When the cloud is almost over the river, we can make out the forms of the individual animals. It's a massive herd of buffalo—a herd that seems to extend for miles and quakes the plain as it pounds toward water."

Bobby sits watching her profile as she talks, admiring

her high cheeks, her abundant hair swept back from her forehead. He could sit and just listen to her for hours. He has been nursing the whiskey, not really drinking it, not wanting to dull his senses. He leans forward, grasping the bottle by the neck and resting it between his knees. "Where do you get these stories? Are you making all this up?"

She doesn't answer, but turns to look straight at him, and says, "Now, this is the bad part." Her voice lowers again and she turns to stare out the window. "We've heard about this other tribe from the Nebraska territory, except it wasn't called that then. I don't know what we called it. Anyway, this tribe calls themselves 'men of men.' They're the Pawnee, and they are big and mean and are great warriors. They don't usually send war parties or hunting parties very much south of the Platte River, but our scouts have spotted a large band of their warriors riding just north of here. The bad part is, they are vicious, and they're the only Great Plains tribe that performs human sacrifice. They usually choose a maiden—you know what that is, don't you?"

Bobby smiles. "Don't know that I've ever met one, but I think I get the idea." He lifts the bottle in salute, then takes another sip. He thinks she might be trying to be cute, talking about the ancient sacrifice of virgins on this spot that has become a parking place for lovers. She just frowns at him.

"Anyway, they choose a maiden and offer her up as a sacrifice to the Morning Star. The ceremonies start with the first thunderstorms of spring and are supposed to bring an abundant corn crop. The big ceremony, though, is the one where they kill the virgin, and they do that around the time of summer solstice. That's bad news for us because it's almost that time of the year, and the crops haven't done well so far this season. And the hunting must be bad in their own territory for the Pawnee to be drifting this far south. But the bad thing is, we are both young virgins from this weakling tribe, and the Pawnee are getting closer and closer."

Bobby pipes up, "Hey, who says?"

"I say." April levels a glare at him in the dimming glow of her cigarette. The approaching storm is almost upon them now, and a flash of light knifes the western sky, illuminating the interior of the car. A few seconds later, there is a low rumble.

"So this is what happens. We are young virgins, and we're just minding our own business working in our mothers' garden over there on the south side of the hill, where it starts to slope gently. We have some corn and beans and some squash. It's almost midmorning, so it's not too hot yet, and many of the men are out of the camp hunting small game. We are just going along and suddenly we hear these screams and we see our people running back and forth in the camp, even running through the fires and falling all over one another. Even the men are screaming and falling, and arrows are flying—just zipping right into the stretched skin of our huts. Then warriors on horseback thunder down out of the woods and crisscross the camp, back and forth, knocking people down. I see a horse charge into my mother as she's running toward me, trampling her. She is moaning and twitching in the dust and I think she's dying and I try to run to her, and I'm screaming now." April takes a quick, nervous puff from her cigarette.

"Just as I'm about to reach her, to throw myself on her, a huge warrior flies from the back of his horse, grabs me around the neck in the crook of his arm, and drags me to the ground. I'm screaming and spitting and trying to bite him, but he pins me to the ground between his knees and holds my wrists with his hands. He is heaving and sweaty and is grotesque in his war paint and his hornlike hair. His scalp lock is stiffened on top of his head with some kind of paint and animal fat so it looks like a horn, and the stench is almost unbearable. He smells of rancid oil and smoke, and his skin is slick with grease. He wears only a loincloth—even his feet are bare. I keep trying to bite his wrists. Suddenly, he lets go with one hand, reaches behind him, and brings out a large hunting knife. He raises it above my head, and when I scream again, he brings the handle and the butt of his hand down hard, right across my cheek. All I see is light. Flashes and flashes of light."

Bobby has been watching her steadily, watching her lips move, her fists clench and unclench. Now he blinks and breaks off the stare. "So, what happened?" he says, his own hands twisting nervously at the neck of the bottle.

April takes the bottle and tips it far back for a long drink. She coughs and has to clear her throat to speak. "They killed me, of course!" She looks into Bobby's face, perplexed that he would need to ask. "They built a platform right here on King Hill and tied me to a rack, spread-eagle, just like that." She stretches her arms and spreads her legs. "Then they shot me with arrows, just like a firing squad. But first the shamans did some incantations and mumbo jumbo over the arrows, so the sacrifice would be good." She crushes her cigarette into the ashtray in the armrest. "The bad thing about the arrows, though, is it wasn't always a fast and clean way to go. I mean, you seldom got a real clean heart shot, or one through the eye right to the brain. A lot of times they would just glance off the bones. The soft spots are where they would really sink deep, all the way to the shaft. They would sink deep in my thigh, in my stomach. My bowels might start to seep out if I got hit down low there. My shoulder maybe. Some might sink deep there and pin me to the rack like a butterfly." She had begun in a matter-of-fact tone, but now she starts to falter. "But the ones in the throat," she says quietly. "The ones that split your windpipe just like a pea shell. Those are the ones I really hate." She turns toward Bobby again, her eyes watering now and her voice beginning to quiver, and puts a finger to her throat. "Right there. That's what I would really hate. That would be the bad part, not being able to breathe because some goddamn son of a bitch put an arrow through your throat." She sinks down in the seat, pressing her hands between her knees, hunching her shoulders, and sniffs back tears.

Bobby blinks again, his own eyes watering from smoke and emotion, his mouth drooping open. "Jesus, April! Don't get so worked up about it. It's just a story, right?"

A tear hangs from her upper lip, and she looks up at him blankly, as if puzzled that someone could be so ingenuous. More lightning crackles above them, a quick series of flashes that are not yet at full force, but are more like the auroras that might be seen by a northern tribe.

"I found her," she says quietly.

"Found who?"

"My mother. I was the one who found her when she killed herself."

Bobby is dumbstruck and is silent for an uncomfortably long time. When he finally speaks, he offers up weak sympathy in an uncertain tone, trying to cast ahead in his mind to where such a confession might lead. "Jeez," he says. "I'm sorry. I didn't know." He truly does not know what else to say.

"I just tell people that she died, but that's what happened." She sets her jaw and stares out the window again. "My father was leaving us. He was a high school teacher in Grand Island and he was in love with a student teacher from

Benedictine College and he was going to leave us and my mother just couldn't stand it, I guess." She stops and turns her streaked face to Bobby's. "How can one person have that much power over another person? Do you know?"

Bobby hesitates, unsure whether the question is rhetorical. After another awkward pause under April's level gaze, he shakes his head and looks down. "I don't know. I just don't." She still stares at him. Suddenly, almost directly above them, the black sky pops, then explodes with a flash that illuminates the hill as if it were midday. April jumps and moves closer to Bobby, and the storm starts in earnest on the hill.

Bobby puts his arm around her shoulder tentatively, silenced by how incredibly innocent his own life has been and intimidated by the strength he now feels coiled in the seat next to him. He feels himself a weakling by comparison.

"I've never talked about this with anyone besides Grandma, you know. Not the details anyway." More lightning rips the darkness. "She just took a load of laundry to the basement one day and didn't come back up. No goodbyes. No tears. Nothing. When suppertime came, I went to look for her and there she was." April stiffens beneath Bobby's arm and examines her hands resting flat against her thighs. She rubs the back of one hand nervously and her voice cracks. "She used a clothesline rope. She pushed herself from the top of my father's pool table." April shakes her head and smiles almost imperceptibly. "My old man really loved that pool table." She takes one more long, steadying drink of the whiskey.

"But this is the bad thing," she says, not looking up at Bobby, but staring at her own hands. "The thing I really hated was her fingers. Her neck was all covered with streaks and gouges, and her fingers were all bloody and purple where she'd managed to slip them under the rope. They were just stuck there, all purple under the edge of the rope. She just decided too late that the son of a bitch wasn't worth dying for."

Bobby feels sour bile rising in his throat, stinging his nostrils. His hands shake as he takes the bottle from April. Desperately, he washes the taste back down and sputters, "Jesus, April! Jesus." Now April is silent, and more thunder rumbles behind them. She stares alternately at her hands and out the window.

Then she takes one of his hands in hers and says calmly, "Just do me a favor. No, two favors. Stop saying 'Jesus' about everything. That doesn't sound nice. And don't tell me how much you love me and how much you want to *show* me you love me. Don't just throw that word around like it's just a word and you know what it is and how to use it. Sex is one thing, but love is more dangerous. It has power—the kind of power thunder tells us about. Some people never learn how to handle it."

April taps out another cigarette from the pack and rolls down the fogged window for some fresh air. The thunder rolls behind them now, somewhere over the parkway, and enormous, water-bomb drops of rain begin to pat the dust around them. Then the sky opens, and the dry hill is awash with the kind of spring shower that dumps everything at once and then moves on. The window handle sticks, and by the time April can get it rolled up, she is soaked. She spits and laughs and tosses her soggy Old Gold onto the floorboard. "We should quit smoking these things anyway." She leans back in the corner of the seat and smiles, her eyes hooded. "Come and just hold me," she says, and pulls Bobby toward her. "No, wait. This is wet." She sits up, crosses her arms in front of her, and peels her T-shirt over her head.

Then she leans back in the seat and pulls him gently to her. He buries his face between her silken breasts, and she strokes his hair with both hands. For now, she feels safe and doesn't want to break away. He wraps his arms around her, wedging them between the fuzzy seat and her warm back, trying to position them in a way he hopes is comfortable to her. He lies perfectly still, trying to make himself feel light and breathing softly against her skin. His mind drifts lazily between her touch and her words, settling on that which is more solid. His concentration narrows to her heart drumming against his cheek, to her fingers playing lightly across his neck, and he wonders how anyone could know more about the words to describe this than he and April do right now. Even in twenty years, they may not know any more than they do at this moment. But for now, he never wants to move from where he is, he never wants the rain to stop, and he never wants to forget what the thunder said. He doesn't see how anybody could.

The Casaloma

RICKEY LEE BABER disliked a lot of things, sometimes for good reasons and sometimes for reasons he couldn't really name. For instance, he especially disliked the Casaloma, although no specific event had triggered his disdain for the place. He just knew that he didn't like the building, and he didn't like the people who congregated there.

He thought there were some things about the place that just weren't right. For one thing, someone told him that the name "Casaloma" meant "house of clay," but as far as he could tell, the place wasn't made of clay at all. Besides that, Rickey Lee just couldn't understand why black folks would want to have a tavern in the middle of a white neighborhood.

The Casaloma was a low, concrete block building with a facade of glazed, deep indigo tiles. It had a heavy, windowless metal door and two small, crank-operated windows in the front. When the windows were cranked half-open, with the bottoms of the panes slanting out and the tops slanting in, the front of the building looked like a lethargic blue face that stared with heavy black eyes out onto the litter-filled street. The Casaloma was one of the few remnants of the old "Blue Town." Years ago, for reasons now unknown, businessmen along two blocks of Market Street in Westgate, Missouri got together and decided that all the buildings in the neighborhood should be blue. The section of town was dubbed "Blue Town," but now all that remained of the blue buildings were the Casaloma and a few others—including the apartment building where Rickey Lee lived.

Rickey Lee lived alone in a room over a nonprosperous insurance agency. The black and gold lettering on the front window of the insurance office was peeling and said "DON ZYKO I SUR NCE, Ind pendent Age t." On the first day of every month, Don Zyko would knock at Rickey Lee's door at midmorning, even though he knew that Rickey Lee had just gotten off work and was probably sleeping. When Rickey Lee opened the door, Zyko would be leaning against the wall, smiling a crooked, smoke-stained smile and wearing a white shirt with yellow stains under the arms.

"Well, Mr. Baber," he would say, "it's that time of the month." He smelled of smoke and alcohol and his breath was warm and rotting. Every month, Rickey Lee felt like stuffing the rent money down his throat, and every month, he thought that if the dump of a room wasn't so close to his job, he'd move. He had been thinking the same thing every month for the seven years he had lived there—ever since he and his grandmother moved there from their apartment on King Hill Avenue. Even now that she was gone, though, he had never gotten around to doing anything about it.

Rickey Lee worked nights at the Rainbow Donut Shop, across the street from the Casaloma. On hot summer nights, groups of young blacks stood outside the bar, some standing down in the deserted, wide street, laughing and waving their arms, strutting in place, and poking fingers at one another then jumping away. Old black men sat on folding chairs around the front door and smoked nubby, filterless cigarettes down to a glow at their fingertips. They leaned forward in their chairs, elbows on knees, hands crossed in front of them, and shook their shoulders with a quiet, hissing laughter, as if there were an old secret humor that they shared with each other, but not with the young men.

Sometimes the black men and women sat on the tops of cars out in the street and played loud music on car speakers until three or four in the morning. The toothy women drank wine from bottles and had shrill laughs and loud voices. Rickey Lee could hear them above the churning of the dough mixers and the pop and sizzle of the deep fryer. He would stand at the wide vat of the hot liquid grease of the fryer, staring at his soft, white hairless arms, sometimes thinking of nothing, and sometimes hating the smell of the burning grease and the sound of the low, deep vibrations from the bass speakers across the street.

The night of the shooting, Rickey Lee walked to work as usual. It was a hot night, and the humidity gave the streetlights misty halos. Across from the shop, small groups of black men stood around the front of the Casaloma, no more or no less than usual. The music coming from within the bar wasn't loud, though.

Larry Jones, manager of the donut shop, was already at work when Rickey Lee arrived. He stood at a long table pounding and folding a flour-dusted mound of dough. His white apron was stained with crusted cream and grease and, here and there, splashes of raspberry jelly.

"Hey, Rickey Lee, the natives don't seem too restless tonight," Larry said. "Maybe we need to throw a fish on the sidewalk and watch the old farts fight over it. Liven things up a little."

"Yeah, you do that, Larry," Rickey Lee said. "Those old boys will kick your skinny ass up between your shoulders." Larry sneered, showing his pointed, rodentlike teeth. Then Rickey Lee noticed that Larry had shaved off his irritating, wispy mustache. "I see you finally wiped the shit off your lip."

"Yeah, I think I'll go with a full beard next time," said Larry. "The chicks will really go for it."

"Too bad you don't have any hair on top. You could comb it down to cover your whole face."

"Screw you," Larry said, and wiped sweat from his face with his bare forearm. Larry's short-sleeve dress shirts always sagged with perspiration and his elbows were dirty from leaning on the sticky desk in the corner of the shop. He was the dough man—the person who mixed the ingredients and ran the dough mixing machines. Rickey Lee was just the fryer and dishwasher, a thirty-year-old doughnut fryer, and Larry never let him forget it. The main thing Rickey Lee didn't like about Larry, though, was that Larry was his friend. He was the person he had to talk to for maybe eight or ten hours a day. Rickey Lee hated having a friend that he didn't even like, but then, he thought, at least Jones was somebody to talk to. At least this way he had a best friend. He wasn't sure how else to go about it anymore. They traded a few more insults, then Rickey Lee began work.

He had just started to scrape down the doughnut glazer with a mason's trowel when he heard the noise from across the street. The dough mixing machine groaned and rattled behind him, the dough pounding and flapping against the stainless steel interior. Then there was a faint cracking noise—crack, crack, crack. The shots broke the steady, thudding rhythm of the mixer. There were shouts from the direction of the Casaloma.

Larry went to the front of the store, then came back in a few minutes. "Looks like we got us some excitement over there now," he said. "Couple of the niggers tried to kill each other off."

"No kiddin'?" Rickey Lee said. "Let's go have a look." They wiped their hands and tossed their aprons on the desk. Rickey Lee's skin tightened with a chill of excitement and a sense of authority. They probably would be the first white men on the scene, so their presence would be something of an official visit—to assess the damage, to judge right and wrong, to make pronouncements about what should happen to those who were responsible.

The front door of the Casaloma was wide open, and the yellow, smoky light from inside threw a bright wedge across the sidewalk and out into the street. In the light of the sidewalk, Rickey Lee could see the spatters of blood, so bright they looked like splashes of paint. Several young men sat weeping on the curb out front, their feet down in the gutter, their folded arms and their heads on their knees. The old men stood near the door, leaning on the backs of their chairs with one hand and letting their cigarettes hover near their mouths with the other, just watching through the door and waiting for the commotion to be finished.

Just inside the door and to the right, on the floor near the end of a pool table, lay the body of a young black man in a pool of blood that ran from a hole in the side of his neck. The blood outlined his body as it flowed around the edges of his clothing and settled to the lowest points in the uneven floorboards. A large man, wearing an apron and yelling orders to others, was already pulling a yellow cotton jacket up over the face of the dead man. Then two police cars with flashing blue lights, but no sirens, slid to the curb in front.

"It was Mickey Jones that done it!" one of the blacks

yelled as the police got out of their cars. "Mothuhfuckuh snuck on him and just ran," another said, pointing down the street. One of the boys who had been crying at the front curb looked up and yelled, "It was cigarettes! They were fightin' over cigarettes, and the son of a bitch just up and shot him."

Rickey Lee and Larry watched from near the front door. The dead man's legs lay scissors fashion, with the top leg thrown over the bottom leg and bent at the knees, as if he were poised to run or to do a break dance on the floor. He wore silk socks and new snakeskin shoes. The real leather soles of the shoes were barely scuffed.

"Look at those shoes," Larry said in a low voice, leaning in close so Rickey Lee could smell his perspiration. "Doesn't it make you wanta puke?"

"What in the hell are you talking about?" Rickey Lee said.

"The shoes," Larry said. "Look at them. Must cost a hundred and fifty bucks, maybe two hundred. And him nothing but a snot-nose kid spade with a momma that's probably on welfare."

"Jeez, what's the matter with you, Larry?" Rickey Lee said. "Keep your voice down or they're gonna hear you. Shit, man, the kid's dead. Can't you leave his shoes alone?"

Larry laughed his nasal twang laugh and shook his head. He gave Rickey Lee a sneering smile and looked him up and down. "Yeah, I'll leave his shoes out of it. I'm not the one who should give a shit about what kind of shoes he's wearing. I'm not the one that wore goddamn raveling Hush Puppies to my granny's funeral." He looked down at Rickey Lee's feet and laughed again.

Rickey Lee flushed red and wanted to pin Larry's neck to the wall with his forearm. The heat of his embarrassment, a building rage, seemed to shift around quickly to different parts of his body. It arced from himself to nearby objects like power from a downed high-tension electrical wire looking for a ground. It jumped from him to his shoes, to Larry, to the dead black man and his shoes, and to the glazed blue tiles of the Casaloma. He shifted his weight and moved his toes around inside his dirty, frayed Converse high-top sneakers.

"Hey, I've got better shoes than this," Rickey Lee said, feeling foolish even as he said it, and hating Larry for the feeling. Larry just smiled and turned to walk toward the police.

Rickey Lee yelled after him. "You and your whole family are ignorant, you know that?" Larry just pretended that he didn't hear.

He worked silently the rest of the night, acknowledging Larry's questions and orders with grunts. He kept his mind to his work and tried to concentrate on flipping the doughnuts and twists in the hot vat of grease just at the right time, quickly, so they would be a uniform golden brown. He tried to concentrate hard, tried to drain his head of thoughts of Granny, the woman who had raised him. Her things were still there in the apartment—even her sausage grinder. He tried to empty his brain of thoughts of how lonely he had been since she died, of how she had been his only friend for years after the accident. He emptied his head of the accident, and the flipper paddles flew in his hands as he cooked batch after batch of doughnuts.

Larry reported about the comings and goings from across the street, and by about three in the morning the police and ambulance and everyone else had gone.

By seven in the morning, Rickey Lee had turned out dozens of doughnuts, twists, fritters, and cinnamon rolls.

After all the batches were loaded into the display cases in the front of the shop, Rickey Lee sat down with a few construction workers who stopped by regularly for warm glazed doughnuts. The construction workers had coffee, and Rickey Lee had a Dr Pepper.

"I'm surprised there ain't been more shootings and stabbings and whatnot over there," one of the workers said. "Wonder what they was fighting over."

"Cigarettes," Rickey Lee said with a mouthful of doughnut. "They were fighting over cigarettes."

"Hell of a thing," one of the workers said, shaking his head. "Hell of a thing." And they all agreed. Rickey Lee chewed the warm, sweet dough and wanted to say more—that it was more than just a hell of a thing. His thoughts were soft, though. Unformed. He had seen briefly into the world that he didn't trust, and he had seen a young man, a boy really, whose life had drained from a hole in the side of his neck. The boy's friends cried for him. He saw a grotesque reflection of himself in a man who couldn't see beyond the dead boy's shoes. He saw a memory there, too—a memory of what it felt like to be young and to see a young friend dead. Death, for your first time, is a hell of a thing, he thought. The mouthful of dough got in his way. "Hell of a thing," Rickey Lee said. It came out "Hehwuvafeng."

After the construction workers left, and as Rickey Lee was wiping off the table where they had been sitting, a young woman walked into the shop and sat at a table away from the sunlight that now glared through the floor-to-ceiling windows along the east side of the building. She had mid-length blonde hair that she pushed back from her forehead, and she wore large, white-rimmed sunglasses. From what Rickey Lee could see of her below the glasses, he could tell she was very attractive—strikingly so, like someone you would see in a magazine or walking briskly through an airport in a big city. She ordered coffee and one doughnut from Imogene, the counter lady at the shop after seven. She took off her glasses, lit a cigarette and looked over her shoulder at the Casaloma. She just stared, as if she were trying to see right through the dense, bolted front door.

Larry came to the front of the store to tell Imogene something. He saw the young woman and started to talk in a loud voice, punctuated with laughter and what he must have thought was an edge of authority. He gave furtive glances toward her table to see if he had her attention, but she continued to stare at the tavern across the street. Larry took the pot of coffee from the Bunn-O-Matic warmer and walked over to her table to give her a refill. "Guess you might have heard, we had a little excitement over there last night," he said. "Had us a little shooting."

She glanced at him briefly, then looked back out the window. "Yes, I heard about it," she said flatly.

"Terrible thing, terrible thing," Larry said. "It's a good thing nobody was hurt—just a spade killed." He laughed his high-pitched nasal giggle and watched her out of the corner of his eye as he walked back to the counter. Rickey Lee reddened and kept his head down as he wiped the counter, feeling awkward in his dirty T-shirt and sneakers in the presence of the woman. She just stared, as if she hadn't heard Larry, but her hand shook as she brought her cigarette to her lips. She pushed her cup of coffee away with the other hand.

Rickey Lee was taking some of the empty trays out of the display case when he saw a tall black man walk past the long windows along the east sidewalk and come to the door of the donut shop. By the time the man had reached the door, Rickey Lee remembered who he was. It was Bill Calloway. Willie is what they had called him back in high school. He was even taller than Rickey Lee remembered, and was dressed in a fine charcoal suit with a light blue shirt and small-pattern tie. He carried himself with confidence, like an athlete, and smiled faintly when he saw the young woman seated in the shop. He walked directly to her table.

"I called Momma," he said to the young woman. "Told her we just drove in and stopped for coffee." His voice was smooth and firm.

"Is she all right?" the woman asked.

"I think so," he said. "She said ladies from church are already bringing food in this morning."

"Well, I don't want to finish this," she said, nodding at her coffee and doughnut. "Let's get out of here and go see your mother."

Rickey Lee watched the couple from behind the counter. He thought Bill had looked in his direction when he came in, but he wasn't sure. He hadn't acknowledged him, so Rickey Lee hesitated before he decided to call out his name. He also hesitated over which name to call out. "Bill" is what Calloway went by when he played basketball at Syracuse and later, when he played pro ball for a time in Kansas City. Rickey Lee had read about him in the papers. But "Willie" is what they had called him back in school, and Willie had always been kind to Rickey Lee.

"Willie, how ya doing, man?" Rickey Lee said across the counter.

Bill's hands were clasped together on the table in front of him, and he left them there as he turned to look at Rickey Lee. One corner of his mouth came up in a slight, tilted smile, and his eyes had a glazed look, as if someone were trying to explain something to him that he didn't quite understand. "I'm sorry," Bill said, "do I know you?"

Rickey Lee paused for a flustered moment. "Yeah, man,

sure you do," he laughed. "Rickey Lee—Rickey Lee Baber. We used to sit at the same worktable in shop class."

"Oh, yeah, I'm sorry," Bill said. "It's been a long time." But Rickey Lee could tell by Bill's dull, searching glance that he still didn't quite recognize him. Bill studied him only for a moment, then let his stare settle, not on Rickey Lee, but somewhere over his shoulder, as if he were transfixed by a spot on the wall behind Rickey Lee.

"Yeah, it's been a long time," Rickey Lee said. "I read about you playing ball and whatnot and being on TV and all in Kansas City."

"Yes, it's been a while," Bill said. "So, how is it going with you?"

"All uphill and stony, Willie, all uphill and stony." There was another awkward pause. "So, what are you doing in town, man?"

"Kind of an emergency. My brother was killed last night." Bill seemed to forget what he was going to say next. "Right across the street there." His voice became thick and whispery, as if he needed to clear his throat, and he gazed vacantly out the window in the direction of the low blue building across the street. The blonde woman put her hand on Bill's folded hands and glared at Rickey Lee, as if he were guilty of Larry's indecencies by association.

Then Rickey Lee smiled involuntarily, not because he thought it was funny but because he didn't know what else to do. He had nothing to say to the woman in his defense, and he had nothing to say to Bill that would mean anything to him. He smiled instinctively, defensively, as if to absorb the impact of something that he couldn't quite name but that he could feel in his jaws, far back in his teeth, burning down into his throat. With his stupid, pinched grin frozen on his face, he groped around in the back of his head for something to say. The young woman saw him smiling, and the color drained from her face and lips.

"Honey, let's go—let's get out of here," she said. Bill turned away from the window, and Rickey Lee's smile dropped.

"Shit, Willie, I had no idea," Rickey Lee said. "I'm sorry, man. I was over there last night when the cops were there and all, but I had no idea it was your brother. Damn." Rickey Lee's own voice had become thick now.

"He was just a kid," Bill said. "Just a kid fighting over who knows what."

"They say it was cigarettes," Rickey Lee said. "Couple of the other boys say they was fighting over cigarettes."

Shining paths of tears trailed down Bill's dry, black cheeks, and he shook his head slowly. "Cigarettes," he whispered to himself.

Bill and the woman rose slowly, as if they were unsure their legs would hold them now, and she put on her sunglasses. "Gotta go now, Rickey Lee," Bill said, collecting himself, wiping his face with the back of his huge hand. "You take care."

"Yeah, you too, man. I'm sorry. I had no idea."

Larry came back to the front of the store just as Bill and the woman were leaving, and suddenly Rickey Lee knew that all it would take would be one word, just the wrong look. Larry kept his eyes on the couple as they walked past the windows and around the corner, their arms looped around each other's waist. "Well, I'm a son of a bitch," Larry huffed. "Don't that make you sick? I would have drank her bath water and there she goes with an uppity nigger."

"Just shut up, Larry!" Rickey Lee snapped. "Just shut your mouth. You're always running off about things you don't know a damn thing about."

"Now, hold on there, buddy," Larry said.

"I'm not your buddy! Just leave me the hell alone."

Larry just laughed at him and walked away.

Rickey Lee's hands shook as he started to polish the glass of the display cases for what he knew would be the last time. He rubbed the glass in large circular motions with newspaper soaked in vinegar, then wiped it with dry paper. As he rubbed and rubbed, he thought of Bill Calloway and the woman and what they would say to each other about him. He thought about the look on her face when she saw him smile, and he thought about the dead boy under the jacket, about hot grease, about Larry.

He wondered if Calloway even remembered the thing that had made him smile involuntarily, the thing that made him want to smile and cry and scream all at the same time every time he thought of it. The unfairness of it made his throat burn and his teeth hurt, and made him smile the worst kind of smile every time he remembered, so he always tried to keep his mind drained of it. Maybe Calloway was away at school by then, so he wouldn't have been one of the ones to blame him. Besides, it wasn't all his fault, he thought. He swears it was something other than the beer that made him swerve like that with his truck. And he told Virgil that over and over again when he found him lying in the dusty ditch, all covered with little diamonds of glass. He screamed it at him as he held him in his arms, his friend's neck snapped just like the telephone pole, the red life draining from its jagged windshield gash onto the shadowed weeds and gravel. After that, they had all given him that look of blame, like the way the blonde woman had looked at him this morning. Disgust and hate, pure and simple. He thought of how long it had been since he had seen that look. How many years? Mostly now it was indifference—just blankness, the way Bill Calloway had looked at him.

Then he thought about the viaduct north of "Blue Town," and how it had always been a kind of imaginary barrier between his neighborhood and the rest of the world, beyond which he didn't venture without a reason. He had had plenty of reason years ago to leap that barrier, but he had been young, and there was Granny still living. Now, though, he saw a reason in the glass. He saw his own reflection as he bent to clean the inside of the display case, the pale reflection of a solitary cartoon character with thinning, greasy hair and a heavy, humorless face. And through moisture that might have been sweat or tears that refused to shake loose from his lashes, and through the vinegar-smeared glass of the display case, he saw the Casaloma. It was just an indigo blur in the glare of the sunlight refracting through the wet glass, so that if he had never seen the Casaloma before, he wouldn't have been able to tell what kind of a place it was, or what kind of people it contained. He simply would have seen that it was blue.

Windows

VIRGIL RYALLS was glad he hadn't worn a shirt when he rode his motorcycle to the drugstore to see Leon Sherman about the job. It made him feel more in control, as if he couldn't be intimidated by this man—this property owner with a beer paunch and watery gray eyes—who might offer him a job even though he might be put off by Virgil's dark, shoulder-length hair and his bare, taut shoulders and stomach. It was as if Virgil were offering him a dare.

"Are you sure this kid will be all right?" Virgil overheard Leon asking old man Sherman behind the counter. Virgil stood at the other end of the Formica counter sipping a cherry Coke. Sammy Sherman, Leon's father, owned the drugstore, and Leon owned apartment buildings that were in need of paint and repairs. That was the job Virgil was there to find out about. Old man Sherman must have been reassuring, because Leon walked over and breathed mints on Virgil, telling him to meet him at the apartment building just off of Noyes Boulevard at nine the next morning. He would show him what needed to be done then.

"You'll be painting with Sherwin-Williams," Leon said.

"Who?" Virgil said, smiling past the straw that rested on his lower lip.

"It's a kind of paint," Leon said. "Top of the line."

"Paint's paint," Virgil shrugged, looking past Leon, letting his eyes roam the mirror behind the counter.

"Paint ain't paint," Leon said. He looked to his father again pleadingly, asking with his eyes and open palms whether the old man really thought Virgil could be trusted to do this important maintenance work.

The old man just shook his head and smiled. Then he looked toward Virgil, eyeing him up and down, and said, "Like father, like son."

"What?" Leon said.

"Nothing," Sammy said, looking toward Virgil again. "Virgil, don't put Leon on too much. He's very serious about his property. Property ain't just property, and paint ain't paint." Then the old man waved them both out with a crooked, pale hand.

Virgil knew he was getting the job because of his dead father, because Sammy Sherman knew his mother and father from way back and had made a special point of calling Virgil's mother when Leon had mentioned the job to him. Virgil smiled to himself when he thought about Sammy's "like father, like son" remark. It made him feel older and dangerous, like he was flying toward something. Even though he was only fifteen years old, he had been riding a motorcycle and driving a car since he was thirteen—since the year after his father's death. Somehow, the police had never caught him, and his mother had been unable to stop him. She seemed almost afraid to try to stop him. It was as if she could pretend that it wasn't a problem.

Sheridan Ryalls, Virgil's father, used to act and dress as

if he still lived in the fifties—with his leather jacket, wavy duck ass hair, and his Levi's jeans pressed, creased, and rolled from the tops of his oxblood penny loafers. He was thirty-eight in 1967, when his gold-flecked Triumph 650 folded like a toy against the side of a Dr Pepper truck that failed to yield the right-of-way. There was a little insurance money and a few death benefits from the meat-packing plant, where Virgil's father had worked on the kill floor stunning hogs before their bristles were singed off. And Dr Pepper paid Virgil's mother a little something in a settlement, even though the insurance men made some noise about his father's drinking. So they weren't destitute. They could keep the little three-bedroom brick house on Harmon Street in the south end of Westgate, Missouri, where Virgil lived with his mother and his older sister, Cheryl. They could use whatever extra money was available, though. So Virgil's mother had been glad to get the call from Sammy Sherman.

Virgil slept late the morning he was to start the job, and he pulled up to the front of the apartment building in his DeSoto at nine-thirty. Leon was there waiting, leaning against a porch pillar with his arms crossed in front of him. Virgil let the car glide to a stop in the mottled shade beneath two huge elms that grew between the sidewalk and the curb. He goosed the engine a little before he switched it off, and blue-white smoke kicked out of the exhaust. The car was an old one, and Virgil's father had fixed it up just a few months before he died.

Virgil sat still for a moment, letting the smoke settle and admiring the shine of the black hood. Then he drew himself out of the car slowly, as if still waking up, and Leon came down off the porch, his arms still crossed.

"Bad sign, Virgil," he said. "Real bad sign. You sure you want to do this job?"

"Yeah. Sure I'm sure." Virgil was shirtless again, wearing Levi's, work boots, and a rubber band to pull his hair back. He laced his fingers and stretched his arms in front of him, limbering up, showing Leon how long and brown his arms were, how solid the triceps and the wrists.

In fact, Virgil wasn't sure he wanted the job. He already felt the cut into his freedom, like an injury that kept him from resting a solid rest. The fact that he had somewhere to be on a summer morning had snagged at him like a fence as he sped through Hyde Park on his motorcycle the night before. He had been with Smokey and Squeak, their Yamahas and his Honda 350 Motosport ripping up chat and throwing sand as they rounded curves on the parkway too fast and not caring. Smokey was nineteen years old and had a handgun that he waved around once in a while. Squeak was eighteen and had dropped out of school when he was sixteen.

After the park was empty, they left the roadway, their headlights leaping and reaching across the darkness, the front wheels sliding on the moist grass, surprising their arms with little jerks. They found separate paths to the top of the wooded hill that overlooked the park. Virgil's path ascended at a sharp angle past a low oak limb that etched his bare shoulder as he passed and almost knocked him off his bike.

"Son-of-a-bitchin' tree almost got me," he said as the three boys sat straddling their bikes and smoking cigarettes at the top of the bluff. From there, they could look down into the blue light of the closed, fenced public pool at the bottom of the hill.

"Hey, man," Squeak said. "You're bleeding." He pointed at his own shoulder with the hand that cupped his cigarette.

Virgil didn't even look down at the blood.

"Swim?" Smokey said.

"Sure," said Squeak.

"Can't," said Virgil, touching his fingers to his scraped shoulder. "Gotta be somewhere in the morning."

Smokey shrugged, and he and Squeak roll-started their bikes back down the path, putting them in second gear and popping the clutches. Virgil flipped his cigarette butt in their direction, then followed them to the bottom of the hill. It was two o'clock in the morning when they split up near the chain link fence of the pool, where Smokey and Squeak would climb over and swim. Virgil went home then, but he didn't wash the blood from his shoulder until morning.

"What happened to the shoulder?" Leon said as they walked around the apartment building looking at the windows.

"Hurt it," Virgil said.

"I can see that," Leon said. "What happened?"

"You ever ride a motorcycle?"

"No."

"Well," Virgil shrugged. "Sometimes you just get hurt."

They made a complete circle around the building and stood once again on the front sidewalk. The building was a huge old brick house that must have been built during the 1920s—three stories and more windows than Virgil had ever seen in any one house. There were a few tattered screens on windows on each floor, spaced in no particular pattern. The house had been subdivided into two apartments on each floor, accessible by way of the wide oak stairs just inside the front door. Almost identical houses sat on each side and across the alley in back. On the east, the shady side, the buildings were separated by a narrow stretch of moist, cool lawn, spongy with fetid leaves and moss. On the west side, there was an abandoned driveway that was cracked and crowded with tufts of wiry brown grass, the kind that spreads in long, fingerlike shoots.

"So, here's the deal," Leon said. "I give you seven dollars per window to caulk and paint the trim and to build and hang the new screens. Oh, and you need to paint the screen frames, too. Black. I have black for that. Forty-eight windows at seven bucks a window. That's $336 for the job. Can you handle it?"

"No problem," Virgil said, still looking up at the highest windows. He sucked at the inside of his cheek in thought. "Got a ladder long enough for those high ones?"

"That's something we need to talk about," Leon said. "The ladder won't reach some of these on the west and south side. You'll have to get them from the inside. You know, lean out or something."

Virgil looked at him as if he didn't have the answers for easy questions.

"So, I'm going to have to trust you," Leon said, taking a ring of keys from his hip pocket and working at slipping some of the keys from the loop. "I'll give you passkeys to the second and third floor apartments, but you'll have to be responsible. Do you understand? I'll have to be able to trust you not to touch anything, not to screw around with stuff that's not yours. And I'll tell the tenants what you'll be doing, so they'll know you might be coming and going sometimes if they're not home."

"No problem," Virgil said again, and he took the keys.

Virgil spent most of the first day lining up materials, making trips back and forth to the lumberyard for odds and ends that Leon had overlooked. He stacked the wood and set up sawhorses on the shady side of the building, and once in a while he would nod and say "Howdy" to the tenants who came and went. It was almost six in the evening by the time he finished on the first day, and good smells were coming from some of the apartments.

As far as he could tell, the arrangements went something like this: top floor, west side—two single men, in their twenties, who wore sharp suits and shiny shoes and who came home to check their mail at lunchtime; top floor, east side—young couple, maybe students at the college, and the wife was a little overweight; second floor, west side—single woman, maybe in her fifties, who had glasses, heavy arms, and lots of flowers in her windows; second floor, east side—single girl, maybe in her twenties, and cute, with a short skirt and lots of books, who glanced back at Virgil twice while she got her mail; first floor, west side—a couple, both tall and clumsily long-limbed, maybe in their thirties, who slept until midafternoon, then emerged with white skin and white uniforms and drove off in a beat-up old Pontiac; first floor, east side—a little old lady with blue-silver hair, the grandmotherly type, who met the mailman at the hallway boxes to retrieve her mail.

Virgil stored the paint cans and tools in a musty little crawl space under the building and snapped the door closed with a padlock. Then he went home and showered. He ate some ice cream from the carton, then lay across the foldout couch in the cool of the basement, dark except for the flicker of the black and white TV that he turned on low. He let his wet hair hang over the side to dry. He hadn't stared at the ceiling very long before he fell asleep.

He woke as if coming out of anesthetic, prickling and violent, ready to swing at something. His mother was shaking him gently by the shoulder. She said he'd better get up so he wouldn't sleep all day. "Your sister's been gone for an hour already," she said.

Virgil swung at her playfully with the back of his hand, knowing he would miss, and said, "I'm up! Leave me alone."

"Come on—get up," she said. She went around switching on lights, then came back to the foot of the bed. "What happened to your shoulder?"

"Nothing!"

He rolled over on his back and let his head hang off the edge of the bed. He closed his eyes tight against the glare of the lamp, forcing tiny phantom explosions of light beneath his clamped eyelids. He could feel his mother standing there looking down on him, then she walked away. She yelled from the top of the stairs, "Oh, I almost forgot! That Donna girl called last night when you were asleep, but I told her I wasn't going to wake you."

"Thanks a lot," he gargled, his upside-down throat stretched backward and clogged with smoky phlegm, his whiskered Adam's apple almost snagging on the word "lot." He kept his eyes closed until he heard her leave through the front door. Then he opened his eyes again and thought for a while about the cleanness of the world when it was upside down. The white-tiled ceiling of the basement became his floor, void of obstacles or clutter save the lonely light fixture so easily avoided. He imagined himself walking around the barren expanse of his upside-down world—a rugless world, without furniture or gravity, where all things that might be touched were above him, clinging to the floor like bats at rest. He'd have to step up and over to enter the next room. He'd have to go down in order to go up the steps to call Donna. It all seemed too complex, so he didn't move for a while and didn't call Donna. And he didn't arrive at the apartment building to begin the screen construction until almost ten o'clock. It was June 15, and the sun was hot—the kind of hot that made it hard to breathe by noon.

He only worked a few hours a day, so it took him nearly a month to get all the screens put together, the corners mitered and the trim tacked in place just so. He painted the framing a shiny black to contrast with the white which would go on the windows and casements. During that time, he began to see more of Donna, he almost broke Squeak's leg one night with the rear door of his car, and, at least once a week, he roamed through the upstairs apartments while the tenants were out. The couple on the first floor, the folks with the white uniforms, yelled at him for making too much noise with the power saw and hammer in the mornings. They worked at night and tried to sleep during the day. So, much of Virgil's work was confined to the afternoons, with the July Missouri sun beating a tan into him that he thought might never go away.

"So, what are these apartments like?" Donna asked one night as they lay across the bean bag chairs in her basement. They were listening to her *Abbey Road* album for the third time that night. Donna liked the part about the love you take being equal to the love you make.

"I don't know," Virgil said. "They're just these rooms with people's stuff in them. Lots of windows. Lots of sunlight."

"What kind of stuff? I mean, what can you tell about the people that live there?"

"I don't know. Just stuff."

"Well, you ought to be able to tell something from it."

"I don't know. Come see if you want to."

"Will you take me?" she said.

"Sure," Virgil said. Donna reached over and lifted his cigarette from his lip, snubbing it out in a kiln-blasted ashtray that she had made in art class.

Then she pushed her jeans down around her bare feet and rolled over on top of him, her long blonde hair covering him, getting into his mouth so he had to spit it away. Her parents were watching *The Tonight Show* upstairs. After the album stopped, he could hear Ed McMahan's laugh over the breathy yelping noises that rose from the back of Donna's throat when she came. She was very emotional when she had an orgasm, but Virgil was glad that she was able to do that without him having to worry about it—without him having to do anything very complicated. She knew how to take care of herself. Donna was seventeen years old, with wholesome good looks and a drinking problem, and would be a senior at Virgil's high school in the fall. She had been a cheerleader until she was kicked off the squad for smoking. And he had no explanation for why he was with her in her basement with their clothes off.

It had been her idea from the beginning. She said she liked his hair and his weird old car, where she had first come to him at a party that spring. She was slightly drunk and had had a fight with her football-playing boyfriend.

"I've been watching you in the halls at school," she said, as she lay back on his front seat that first night. "Did you know that?"

"No," he said.

"Well, maybe we can just keep it to ourselves," she said.

"OK." He had no idea what else to say as she guided his hands.

Since then, she would call him at odd times of the day or night. Her boyfriend, Ronnie, played a lot of softball during the summer. Sometimes she would call Virgil at eleven o'clock at night to see if he could come over to watch a late movie on TV with her—something in black and white with Humphrey Bogart or Spencer Tracy. Her parents seemed to ignore the late coming and going and the fact that Donna wore shorty pajamas.

One night she called early in the evening to ask if he could come over to watch *The Wizard of Oz*. It started at eight, and they watched it upstairs, with her parents and popcorn. Donna was an only child. Her father wore glasses down at the end of his nose and said two things during the movie. He asked if Virgil wanted more Kool-Aid, and he said, "We used to have one of those DeSotos when we were first married. Good car. Nice old car."

When Dorothy arrived in Munchkin Land, Donna got up in the middle of the living room and sang and danced along with the Munchkin kids from the Lollipop Guild. She screwed up her face and could sound just like them. Virgil didn't say anything, but her mother smiled, clapped her hands together, and said that Donna had always loved that part. After the movie, Donna walked with Virgil down to his car at the end of their driveway.

"What does your old man think about all this?" Virgil said.

"Who knows?" Donna said, pressing against him as they leaned against the car, on the side away from the house. "How's anybody supposed to know what he thinks? He's a CPA."

"What's that mean?"

"Certified Public Accountant," Donna said.

"What's that?"

"Man," Donna said, smiling and shaking her head. Then she guided his hand down the front of her cotton shorts as Virgil looked for movement at the lighted windows of her house.

On the day Virgil took Donna to visit the apartment building, she wore very short jean shorts and a sleeveless T-shirt with no bra. She had permed her hair into crinkly little waves that sprung out around her shoulders like petticoats, and she was letting the hair on her legs and under her arms grow. The hair on her legs was silky and almost white. For some reason, though, she had shaved the hair off her forearms. As they rode along Noyes Boulevard on his motorcycle, she told Virgil to take his free hand and feel how smooth they were. Her sleek brown arms held tight around his waist, and he wished she hadn't come along.

He had been out late the night before, drinking too much wine and eating barbecue at a party in Atchison with Squeak. He didn't know anyone there, and before the night was over, he rode his motorcycle up the front steps and across the front porch of the woman's house, knocking potted plants off as he went. Someone had yelled at him, saying "You shit!" He and Squeak must have gone seventy miles an hour along some stretches of Highway 59 on the way home. And now, the fact that Donna had shaved the hair off her arms made him want to swing an elbow at her.

"Why'd you do that?" he yelled into the wind.

"Just felt like it," she yelled back. "Just something different."

He didn't say anything else, but went too fast around the curves on the parkway, so he could feel Donna stiffen behind him, tightening her arms around his stomach until he thought he might throw up.

When they got to the apartment building, he told her she could sit or she could help. She held the ladder for him as he hauled a can of paint to one of the third-floor windows on the west side. The ladder was stretched as far as it would go. It was the kitchen window for the apartment that belonged to the two bachelors. Virgil knew the place by heart, and he knew their schedule. They wouldn't be in during the afternoon. The grandmother downstairs was home, as was the white-uniformed couple who slept during the day. Virgil painted for a while and scanned the interior of the apartment. After a time, he climbed back down the ladder and said, "You want to scope out the inside of this one?" He motioned with his hand toward the top of the ladder.

"Can you let us in?" Donna said.

Virgil led her around to the front of the building. Even though it was bright outside, the stairwell was windowless and dark.

"Jeez, they need a bulb or something in here," Donna said.

"Quiet," Virgil said as they reached the third floor. He slipped the key into the dead bolt. Then he pushed the door open quickly, letting it ease closed lightly after they were inside.

Donna looked around the room. The front door was near the kitchen, which was off to the right. The kitchen was separated from the living room by a counter with cabinets and a stove. Dishes were put away, and the sink was scrubbed bright white. The chrome on the stove and refrigerator reflected rainbow glints from the clean coffee mugs that hung on hooks along the bottom edge of the cabinets. The plants in the living room had a waxy shine.

"My God, these guys are clean!" Donna said. She walked into one of the two bedrooms, and Virgil followed her. Carpeted runners ran along the hardwood floors and into the walk-in closet. The double bed was taut with a crisp white chenille bedspread. The maple dresser top held some loose change and a gold-framed picture of a girl, perhaps in her twenties, who wore glasses. Beyond that it was clear, polished. Donna went into the bathroom and yelled out, "These guys even do the toilet!"

"Check this out," Virgil said, and pulled the chain for

the light in the closet. Donna looked over his shoulder at the rows of wing-tip shoes and loafers, the racks of sport coats and suit jackets, hanger after hanger of crisp white or pastel shirts.

"Let me guess," she said. "These guys are lawyers."

"They sell suits and shoes at Mr. Guy's," Virgil said.

"You're kidding! This stuff is too conservative."

Virgil raised his hands, palms up, and said, "Well, I've seen them—out at the mall. They were both working at the same time."

"What do they look like?" Donna said.

"They look like these clothes—like this apartment. Squeaky. Short hair, you know. Tapered up the back. One of them wears horn-rimmed glasses and drives a '68 Camaro."

Donna peeked into the other bedroom, which looked almost like the first one, then walked back into the living room, swinging her hips. She went to an end table near the couch and glanced down at the neatly squared stack of *Playboy* magazines there. The July 1970 issue was on top.

"I suppose you've been all through these," she said, picking up the one on top and thumbing through it.

Virgil nodded and said, "They're arranged according to date, with the most recent ones at the top."

"Now, why would I have guessed that?" Donna said. She opened the book to one of the pictorial spreads, holding it right side up, then sideways. She shook her head and said, "Big boobs. Big surprise. Jesus, haven't these girls ever seen themselves before?"

"Maybe we should get out of here," Virgil said.

"Why? They won't be coming, will they?" She tossed the magazine back on the stack, and Virgil came along behind her and squared it up again, so it was aligned with the others.

"No," he said. "But I never know when old Leon is going to come by for a little inspection."

"Let's take something," she said suddenly, turning and looking him full in the face.

"No!" Virgil said. "They'll know who did it."

"Not if it's something small, something they'll never miss."

"Why would you want to do that?"

"Just for the hell of it," she said, eyeing the room.

"I don't think we should."

"Virgil, you surprise me sometimes." He could tell from her tone and the way her face had darkened, taking on a hard crease around her mouth, that she meant he disappointed her sometimes. She took a bent cigarette from a crumpled pack in her back pocket and fished into her front pocket for a match.

"I don't think these guys smoke," Virgil said.

"Well, now shit!" Donna said, rolling her eyes to the ceiling and dropping her hand with the unlit cigarette to her side. "OK, now. That's it. Come with me." She walked back into the bedroom, and Virgil followed. She sat down on the chenille bedspread and pulled her shirt up over her head. She lay back with her arms above her head, the hair under her arms curled into wet little question marks. The shades were thrown wide open, and the light falling across her from the tall windows was startling.

When they were finished, Virgil went to the window and looked out at the apartment building across the alley. He could see an old woman sitting in a chair near an open window, the flicker of afternoon television lighting her pale face. He had to put his hand above his eyes to block the sun. He thought he saw her turn toward him, then look away quickly. Donna sat on the spotless toilet just off the bedroom, watching him, and said, "I think she got an eyeful."

"Let's get out of here," Virgil said, turning from the window quickly and walking into the living room. He went to the stack of magazines on the end table and lifted three out of the middle of the pile carefully, leaving the others neatly arranged, seemingly untouched. Donna stood behind him, and he turned and offered them to her.

"Here, we'll take these," he said. One of them was a Christmas issue with a scantily clad female elf on the front.

Donna laughed and said it was just what she had always wanted.

"Let's just go," Virgil said.

They clicked the door quietly behind them, and Donna put the magazines up under her shirt. Outside, Virgil put the paint and ladder away quickly, without talk, and then they left.

Virgil was rarely home for supper, and he was out of sorts when he ate chicken and rice with his mother and sister that evening.

"How's the window painting going?" his mother asked as she poured more iced tea.

"OK," Virgil grunted, his mouth full of rice. He swallowed and said, "It's taking a lot longer than any seven bucks a window justifies, I'll tell you that."

"Well," his mother said. "Your dad used to say that sometimes the burden can be heavy, but the reward can be light." She smiled when she said it—a smile that irritated Virgil beyond reason. He stopped eating and laid down his fork.

"What's that supposed to mean?" he said.

"Virgil," his mother said, "you know—light."

"Where did he come up with such shit?" Virgil said. He

breathed out quickly, as if trying to rid himself of something, and his own tight little smile was a stab at his mother.

"I don't know," she said, confused now. "He just thought of these things sometimes."

Virgil looked straight at her, something he seldom did. "He was just a drunk sometimes, Mom. He got carried away with himself sometimes. That's all."

She sucked in and said, "Oh!" She put her fingers to her lips to prevent anything else from escaping. Even though his mother was still a young woman—a woman men would find attractive—she suddenly seemed old and frail to Virgil, weakened by his power over her.

His sister, who was good-looking in a medical receptionist sort of way, just blinked at him, her eyes wet with silent anger, and kept pushing things around on her plate. Virgil didn't feel like eating any more chicken, and when his mother said his name softly and moved her hand toward one of his, he pushed himself back from the table and went downstairs to look at the ceiling.

The scraping, sanding, and caulking of the old windows was slow work, and hot, especially on the west side of the building and the side near the alley, where there were no trees. There was just the relentless glare from the afternoon sun, gaining intensity from the reflective bricks and shingles. Up on the ladder, things were just a blur sometimes from the sweat dripping into Virgil's eyes, and his feet felt like that poem he read once, something about apple picking and being able to feel the rungs of the ladder pressing into your arches even after you were done for the day.

Sometimes Virgil would just stop what he was doing in the middle of the afternoon and ride his motorcycle to the wooded bluffs which guarded the east side of the river north of town. He rode to the top, mostly in first or second gear, over last year's paths that had been rutted with the summer's rain. His father had first taken him to the high reaches of the bluffs on the back of his motorcycle when Virgil was only seven or eight. There were a few clearings at the top, some sunlit cuts into the thick oaks and cottonwoods, where he could look out over the river and watch it snake down around a bend that hadn't been there before the 1954 flood. On the other side of the river, the Kansas landscape seemed flattened by the weight of the hazy air that hung over it. Even the buildings in Elwood seemed flattened by the heavy air, none of them taller than two stories.

Virgil could almost make out Moose's Carry-Out store, just off Highway 36 at the edge of Elwood. It was nothing more than a hut really, with glass coolers for the 3.2 beer that could be bought on a Saturday night for $1.25 a six-pack by a teenager who looked eighteen. It had already worked for Virgil. But now, in a way he couldn't really articulate or think about clearly, he was beginning to regret it, as if there was a dirtiness attached to things that came to him that quickly and that easily. He felt bad for even knowing Moose's might be seen from that vantage point. He felt like crying sometimes when he went into the bluffs, yet he kept going back; and he knew that he would never take Squeak and Smokey there. He would rather run into bikers that he didn't know in those hills. They could just nod to one another or give sparse advice about how to climb a particular path. They could just watch the river roll south or watch the sun setting over Kansas in silence and not have to know anything else. He would never take Donna there.

He had taken several trips to the river bluffs after the day he stole the magazines, and sometimes he told Donna he couldn't make it over to see her when she called, even though he didn't have anything else to do. There were fewer softball games at the park as the end of summer drew near, and Donna's boyfriend parked his Impala in front of her house more often. August football practice would be starting, and Virgil thought that Donna would be shaving her legs and under her arms soon, getting rid of the jean shorts and halter tops and going back to her plaid skirts and bright sweaters. She would still drink too much sometimes, but she would act differently toward him once they were back in school. Somehow, he knew it and felt sorry for it.

The day after he had painted the last of the upstairs casements, he was in the side yard of the building, getting ready to haul the last two screens to the top of the ladder. He had on a tool belt and carried a hammer to tap in a nail to start the wood screws for the hangers. He was carrying the screens toward the back of the house when a '68 Camaro slid to a stop at the front curb. The clothes salesmen from Mr. Guy's had come home to check their mail. Virgil wondered what they expected to find there every day. Today, though, instead of walking toward the mailboxes in the front hall, they walked straight toward him, their paisley neckties swinging. They walked briskly, with purposeful strides, and Virgil thought he saw the one in front pumping his closed fist slightly, as if trying to pump up his own adrenaline. Their lips were pinched, ready to offer a deal or an ultimatum. The one with glasses led the way, squinting into the sun, his face red with anger or heat.

Instantly, Virgil knew that they knew. They knew about him and Donna and the chenille bedspread, and they knew about him taking the magazines. He wondered why they would be looking through the middle of the stack. The men coming toward him were bigger than he remembered, broad through the padded shoulders, but he could take both of them out with the hammer if they tried to grab him. The hammer was almost new and had a blonde handle. Sixteen ounces that felt good when it whiffed the air. He tightened his grip on it, swinging it just slightly to feel its weight, and got ready to drop the screens from his other hand if he needed to. He could stun them like hogs, but then he would have to go somewhere.

The men stopped suddenly, though, maybe five feet away, and the one with glasses said, "Hey, kid. Virgil, is it?"

"Yeah," Virgil said, eyeing them.

The man jerked his thumb toward the upstairs window and said, "Listen, Virgil. You painted all our windows closed. Jesus, we couldn't even get the ones with the screens open last night. We just about smothered. Fix them so they open, will ya?"

"Yeah," Virgil said, his heart racing, his air coming in short huffs. "Sorry. I'll fix them."

"Good," the man said, trying to sound authoritative. "We'd like it done by tonight."

"OK."

The two men seemed satisfied and turned to walk away. But the one who had done the talking turned back suddenly, again causing Virgil to grip the hammer, and said, "By the way, the folks down on the second floor said some of their windows were stuck, too."

"OK. Thanks," Virgil said. He had no idea why he was thanking them.

After the two men checked their mail and left, Virgil finished hanging the last of the screens. He walked around the building, inspecting his work, admiring the neatness and contrast of the black on white trimming. Then he went to his car and retrieved the stolen magazines from beneath his front seat. Donna said they should just throw them away, but Virgil had saved them for some reason, even though he hadn't looked at them. Now he carried them out in the open and went to the upstairs apartment. He let himself into the apartment, went to the stack of magazines, and slipped the missing issues into place. Then he went back to clean up the tools, to stack the remaining wood and cans of paint in the cool crawl space under the building, to collapse the ladder and lay it along the foundation at the back of the house.

Before he left, he went back through both of the upstairs apartments to open the windows. He had to pry at some of them with a putty knife, working its blade down around the tacky edges and pulling it back and forth until he felt and heard the pop of sealed, dried paint. He strained at pulling the windows up, his arms shaking sometimes with the effort. He left them all open as far as they would go, and he left the doors to the apartments open into the hallway. Then he trotted to the bottom of the stairs, two steps at a time, and opened the front door of the building, propping it open with an antique iron that someone had painted with pastel tempera paints. Next, he went to the apartments on the second floor, going through all the rooms, pulling up shades and opening windows. He had to pull and pry at some of them, too, and he left the doors to those apartments open. The rooms seemed to exhale huge breaths of light into the hallway.

Virgil went to the second floor landing, almost the architectural center of the building, and bent over, his palms on his thighs, tugging at the edges of his jean shorts as he tried to catch his breath. The warm air rushing through the apartments kicked up a storm of dust and light on the stairs and landing. Smells from all of the apartments met there in the hall, informing Virgil of lives that suddenly made him feel happy. Even though he was tired and dirty, covered with turpentine and sweat, with flecks of chipped paint and dead grass clinging to his moist skin, he felt surprisingly clean. The warm, dry breeze whipping through the wide-open windows began to evaporate his sweat, tightening his skin.

It felt like the kind of clean that he would know years later, when he would lay bricks and see that they were plumb, or when he would admire some other handiwork—something that he felt had been worth the effort. It was the kind of feeling he would get when he'd watch his wife sleep early in the morning—a kind of deep sleep, full of nothing but trust and good intentions. An easy, well-scrubbed sleep. It wouldn't be Donna, but it would be someone he would know within a year. It would be someone who was a little too tall and too thin at that very moment, while he caught his breath in the swirl of the stairway which, perhaps, had never been brighter.

Dead Coach

SHE NEVER should have given up those kids to her ex-husband without more of a fight. That was the first thing Tamma thought of as she pulled herself up from her soggy pillow and dropped her feet over the edge of her cot onto the gritty, cool linoleum floor of the trailer. If she could just be with her kids, she thought, maybe she wouldn't have these dreams that kept waking her and staying with her, making her feel so heavy during the day that she could hardly get anything done. She felt like she was making some progress, and she hadn't had a drink in months. Sometimes she had good days, sometimes bad. But when she remembered her dreams, it was as if the whole day was just shot before it even started. It was as if she had never rested.

She had that one dream again early this morning, and it woke her. She dreamed a lot about the little house they had down at Petersburg, even though she had only lived there for two out of her thirty-six years. In this particular dream, she is in the house talking on the telephone to somebody, and Debbie, her oldest, comes running into the house saying they can't find little Kara and that maybe she should come and help them look. Tamma thinks maybe they are playing some kind of game, so she tells Debbie to wait just a minute until she is off the phone. Can't she see she's talking to somebody? Maybe she's talking to a friend from a few doors down, or maybe she's on a long-distance call. The dream is not really clear on that. Then there is the search, the little electric shock of panic, the overwhelming weight of dread. And then there is the screaming.

Sometimes when she wakes up, her throat hurts from all the screaming she has been trying to do in her sleep. She's soaked with sweat, as wet as if she'd been thrashing around in water. And she feels in a panic, like she needs to call Glenn to make sure the kids are safe.

She doesn't call him, though. She's not supposed to call or visit or take the kids on trips except at the appointed visiting times, and even then it's just for a short time, and they can't go too far. Her old car won't go very far anyway, so it's hard to get down to Richmond for her visits. The old Chevette won't even start now, and it sits outside her trailer all covered with a frosting of icy fog that has descended on the little hollows of Madison County's wedge of the Blue Ridge mountains. One of the back tires on the car is going flat.

Her throat hurt again this morning as she started to move around in the two rooms of her trailer. Sometimes she thought it was from the silent screaming, but sometimes she thought it was from the gas heater that hissed and blew hatefully hot air across the kitchen. The heater just went crazy when she had to turn it on, and it made the trailer stifling, giving the air inside the place a heavy, sick sweetness. It gave her headaches when she would come in from the fresh, cool mountain air to the stale closeness of the trailer. She had had to turn the heat on last night, though, even though it was March and was warm sometimes during the day. At night, down in the folds of the mountains, puddles froze on the hard, packed dirt around the trailer. Now her cheeks burned pink with the heat from the uncontrollable furnace, and her head and throat hurt. She steadied herself against the door jamb, then by the edge of the dinette table against the wall, as she moved slowly into the kitchen to turn off the heat. Her feet were bare on the linoleum, and she wore only her underpants and a large T-shirt, one of Glenn's old ones.

Early gray light started to fill the room, so she knew there was no point in trying to go back to sleep to kill the headache. She wouldn't be able to sleep now anyway because of the dream. She went to the stove to put on water for coffee, and there was a mouse, just sitting on top of the stove, right next to one of the burners, gnawing and chewing at a hard, crusted smear of noodle from the canned spaghetti she had eaten the night before. She threw a rolled magazine at the stove, and the commotion sent the mouse scurrying down into the corner behind the cabinets and out of reach.

After she put on the coffee, Tamma walked down to the road to see if the morning paper had come yet from Charlottesville. She didn't bother to get dressed, but she pulled on a pair of battered running shoes that were next to the door and slipped out into the cold air, hugging herself with her arms. The air was like a reviving slap after the heavy heat of the trailer. She trotted down to the mailboxes, dodging the puddles of turbid ice along the gravel driveway, a portion of which she shared with the main house. The trailer sat on a slope away from the house and through some trees, so it wasn't visible from the road. She pulled the rolled paper from its white tube and trotted back up the drive, her head pounding like a loosely packed box with each jolt. Her arms and legs were tight from the cold by the time she got back to the trailer.

The lights in the main house weren't on yet. Old Mr. Lacy, the lawyer who lived there and whose ailing wife Tamma helped take care of during the day, wasn't awake yet, so she had some time to herself for some coffee. She would go to the main house when Mr. Lacy left for the morning. With coffee and paper in front of her, she sat at the dinette table in her underwear, rubbing her arms and legs. She flipped through the pages to the back of the first section, looking for the entertainment news—which movie stars were doing what—when something on the obituary page caught her eye, made her stop, then pushed the breath out of her as if she had been hit in the chest.

She had to read the obituary over again several times before she was sure it was about him. All the facts were there. All the regular ones anyway. Name, Vincent Morris. Age, 61. Right street address. The tiny biography talked of his coaching boys' baseball. It said he was preceded in death by a son, Lonnie. All those normal facts were there.

Tamma needed to call somebody about it. She wanted to talk to someone who knew him, to verify things, to make sure it wasn't a mistake. She wanted assurances that, like the wicked witch of the east, he was really most sincerely dead. Even though she knew she probably couldn't pay the bill when it came, she decided to call her friend Patti long-distance, over the mountain in Charlottesville. Before she dialed, she took a bent Old Gold from the crumpled pack on the table, lit it, and took several deep, lung-aching puffs to calm herself. She didn't even stop to think that most folks probably wouldn't be out of bed yet.

Patti answered groggily after several rings.

"Did you see the paper?" Tamma said.

"What?"

"Did you see that Coach died?"

"Who is this?" Patti said.

"It's Tamma. Coach died."

"Tamma? Where are you calling from?"

"I'm up here in Madison. I'm calling from my place."

There was silence at Patti's end, a silence filled with the faint vibration and echo of long distance that was comforting to Tamma. The sound of long distance carried weight. It seemed to make her thoughts and words palpable even before they came out, as if the lines hummed in anticipation.

"Did you see the paper yet?" Tamma repeated.

"You woke me up," Patti said.

"You'll see then," Tamma said. "Go get your paper and you'll see."

"We don't even get the paper. I'll have to pick one up at the store."

"Coach died."

"You said that. I'm sorry—I guess, I mean, so why are you calling me about it, Tamma? We haven't talked for forever."

"I know," said Tamma, her hand shaking as she brought the cigarette to her lips again and again. "I just wanted to make sure somebody else knew. I'm sorry."

"I guess a lot of people probably know. Are you OK?"

Now there was silence for a moment at Tamma's end of the line. Then she said, "Yeah, I'm fine. I just. . . Well, good talking to you, Patti."

"What are you going to do?" Patti said.

"About what?"

"Will you come to the funeral?"

"No, I don't think so," Tamma said, and gave a little laugh.

"Well, if you make it down, you be sure to call or come by. OK?"

"Sure thing." She looked around the trailer, as if looking for something else to say. "Well, bye." She pushed the receiver button down with her finger while she still held the phone to her ear. She sat in that position for several seconds before hanging up. It occurred to her then that Patti didn't really know about Coach. Not really. Nobody did.

She got up and walked nervously from the table to the sink, flicking ashes into the stack of crusty dishes, then back to the table again. She made the trip several times, each time flipping ashes and carrying one more dish or cup from the table to the sink, as if one item were all she could carry while she managed the glowing end of the cigarette with her other hand. She wanted to make her next call—to get it over with—but her stomach lurched and her bowels burned when she thought of it. She circled the phone slowly, not looking at it directly, doing other things as she went. She pulled on a pair of jeans that lay across the chair. She pushed back the short white curtains from the kitchen windows, the folds gray with dust, and set off a golden particle storm as the light came streaking through. She knew the number, even though she only called it once a year. She would never forget the number, his number. She was determined to use it again, this time to talk to her, Coach's wife, to tell her what was what, to shift the blame once more for all that had happened, to lance the boil of resentment.

She paced back and forth more furiously, stopping to let her vibrating hands light another cigarette, only to snub it out again quickly. It was probably a heart attack, she thought. Coach's personality meant heart attack. She remembered thinking that about him the first time she saw him. She thought, one of these days, that man is going to explode—just burst every major artery in his body. She remembered the way his nostrils flared and his eyes dug deep, as if flames might shoot out.

Coach was having a fist fight with one of the other fathers the first time Tamma saw him. It was late in the game, and Lonnie had hit a triple in the previous inning. She remembered that. It was the spring she turned seventeen, and the spring she and Lonnie first made love in the back of Coach's 1965 Buick. It was red with a white top and a wine-red interior. She remembered that, too.

She remembered the Morris's little clapboard house in the Belmont section of Charlottesville, the part of town where folks lived if they couldn't afford to live somewhere else, and how Coach used to let things there get run down some and used to let the grass grow a little longer than neatness would allow. But he always kept that Buick shined, bright and hard like a piece of Christmas candy. She remembered Coach's firm, tan arm stretched across the seat top, his shirt sleeve rolled, revealing pale skin above the bicep. His other hand spun the wheel wildly, and he smiled sometimes when Lonnie wasn't around. She remembered the heat of that summer, and she remembered the cool length of Lonnie's smooth body, his bright blonde hair, his long fingers and the way they curved.

Then, November. When the long, cold nights gripped both ends of the short, gray days like a vise holding steel, she said she was pregnant. She said it into the telephone, as if she were calling an ambulance or the police—someone with the skill and authority to care for her. She felt things tumble through the silence. She expected only a little word, a touch. But nothing was offered. When she called again, Coach answered and said, "Don't call here." She ran to the bathroom and vomited into the sink, where her mother found her pounding pink tile with bloodied knuckles.

The rest was like a snowstorm, where things happened, but in a hush. Her trip to the Harrisonburg doctor, an evening visit arranged by her mother. Lonnie's sudden transfer to a Catholic boys' school in Richmond. Then, in February, there was the slick stretch of Broad Street in Richmond. Lonnie was a passenger with two older boys. His side of the car hit the light pole first. There had been some drinking, and conditions were icy.

That's when she lapsed into her trance of grief. She climbed into a cocoon of silence, in which she would just sit and stare, not emerging until spring. And later that summer is when she received the first of the telephone calls.

The man's voice, vaguely recognizable, said, "I saw you going to the swimming pool today in that swimsuit. You know? The red and white one. Two pieces. I like the way you pull the back of it down. Run your finger up under the edge and snap it down."

"Who is this?" Tamma said, even though she knew she should just hang up. Something about the voice made her stay on the line.

The voice said, "I always liked your butt, the way it twitches when you walk. And your calf muscles. He would have liked those."

"Why—," she started to ask, but she was too shocked and confused to even try to cope with the reasons for the call. She remained silent, gripping the receiver hard with one hand, steadying herself on the back of a chair with the other. She recognized the voice, and felt as though she would be sick.

"I told him to be careful, though," the voice said. "Said I'd look for pecker tracks in that car." The man's words were slurred, perhaps by booze or nervousness or depression. "I told him," the voice said. "I told him that being pussy whipped would ruin him. You've got to be careful."

"Mr. Morris," Tamma said, her voice quivering. "Please don't do this. It's not my fault."

"Well, whose is it?"

Tamma let the question go unanswered.

"You told him, didn't you?" she said. "You told him not to talk to me anymore." There was a long pause, as if nothing would ever happen beyond that time and that place on earth. "I got an abortion. Did you know that?" Again, silence.

"Meet me somewhere," Coach said.

"No!"

"Please."

"I can't do that."

"Why?"

"Mr. Morris, this is too strange. Please don't do this."

Tamma had begun to shake so violently she could hardly hold the receiver. Then there was a click on the line, and the steady, pulsing signal that the call was over. She replaced the receiver roughly, sat down, and began to sob. After that day, she let the call, the voice, burn under her like a hot coal that would flare into a spark of hate when stirred by a gust of memory or a cool draft of loneliness. It was as if she could punish herself and him just by remembering the call.

Coach called several more times after that—she knew it was him—but he said nothing. The silence leaned down on her, made the receiver heavy in Tamma's hand, and made her breath come quickly through winged nostrils. Sometimes she would touch herself and then cry. It was after she married Glenn and moved away that she got the idea to reciprocate. She would return the favor. Each year, on Lonnie's birthday, she would call Coach and say nothing. Dead silence. She would just sit, hardly breathing, and let the static echo of the silent call remind the father of lost voices. No matter where she and Glenn and the kids moved over the years, she made her annual call, and she was sure Coach knew who it was and why she was calling. After the first few years, he answered quickly, as if standing ready to protect his wife—or standing ready to accept some sort of blame.

Sometimes she had to call long-distance. Glenn's job moved them from Charlottesville to Spotsylvania, down to Petersburg, and back up to Madison. Now Glenn and the kids were in Richmond. She had to call from the hospital, like the time she was there from one of her miscarriages, and the time Glenn hit her too hard. Once, she had to call from a motel, the time she ran off from Glenn with the four kids. Then last year, before she came to work for Mr. Lacy, she had called from the hospital again. She had to sneak the call, because they wouldn't let her use the phone at that hospital. She was on so much medication at that hospital she could hardly remember the number, could hardly dial it because her fingers felt so thick and full, like tree stumps. She made it, though. She never missed a year.

She was reflecting on her diligence and consistency in making her calls, still sitting at her dinette table, poised and ready to make the call to Mrs. Morris, when she heard the crunch and pop of gravel along the driveway. Mr. Lacy was on his way to town. She would have to go to the main house soon. She would have to make it quick. She crossed her legs, knee over knee, as her index finger dialed. She stood up nervously while it rang. Her teeth were bitter from smoke and cold coffee. She ran her tongue over them and her dry lips, flexed her jaw muscles, ready to speak. She was ready to wake Mrs. Morris up, to tell her something about Coach and punishment and pain that never quits, and to punish her for just sitting by when she might have done something about it. Good Catholic family. She wanted to just spit it all out like it was poison, a final release she could no longer obtain from Coach, another long-distance call she couldn't afford.

The phone rang four or five times before a woman's voice answered.

"Mrs. Morris?" Tamma said.

"No, this is her neighbor, Lois," the woman said. "Mrs. Morris is trying to have a little something to eat. May I help you?"

Of course, Tamma thought. Friends and neighbors will be there this morning, waiting on Mrs. Morris, doing things for her, bringing in food and asking her over and over again to eat it, just try a little of this. She remembered how that was now. Folks had done that for her when her mother passed on—and again later. Still, it was disconcerting that someone else had answered. Tamma was flustered, her concentration was broken.

"I'm an old friend of the family," Tamma said. "I just wanted to give her my sympathies. Just tell her."

"Oh, wait," the woman said. "Here she is." Voices and rustling fabric were muffled by a hand over the mouthpiece.

"Hello," another woman's voice said. "This is Mary Rae."

"Mrs. Morris?" Tamma said, faltering. Her free hand rubbed nervously at spilled salt on the table, grinding it to dust with her fingertips. She had forgotten about all the people who would be there, all the food. She had forgotten that part. She had forgotten how the fancy dishes, the meats and the sweet pies and cakes, will all taste like cotton. Folks will be calling. Folks will be trying to make her eat, when all she wants to do is just curl up in a corner somewhere with something—a shirt, a belt, a book—just a little something left behind that she can latch on to.

"Mrs. Morris, this is a friend." She couldn't think of what to say next, so she said, "Never mind."

"What?"

"I just wanted to call to say—I just called to say some things to you."

"Who is this?"

Suddenly, Tamma thought of old Mrs. Lacy. If she didn't go up to the house soon, the cook would come looking for her, and Mr. Lacy might hear about it.

"Just an old friend," she said, speaking in a breathy rush. "I knew Coach for a long time. I knew Lonnie, too."

"Oh?" Mrs. Morris said, her tone uncertain.

"I've gotta go," Tamma said, her eyes jumping around the inside of the trailer. "I just. . . The doctors say I should quit blaming him. They say he's not the cause of the stuff that's happened to me. I was calling to say some things to you, but I don't know now. Maybe forget it. Maybe they're right. Lots of folks go through a lot and get along okay. My mother had it hard, too. But I don't know."

"Who is this?" Mrs. Morris's voice was beginning to shake. Tamma could hear another woman's voice murmuring something in the background.

"I just know a little of what you're feeling, I guess. I remember. I lost some people, too. One a long time ago, and one just about a year and a half ago. That's when I had to go into the hospital for a long time, and the doctors told me I had to quit drinking and quit blaming everything on him.

I was letting it just eat away at me like it was a cancer or something. They say I need to let things go."

There was the other woman's muffled voice in the background again, and Mrs. Morris said, "I don't know. I can't make heads or tails of it." She sounded puzzled and pleading.

The other woman, her neighbor, came back on the line. "Who is this?" she demanded.

Tamma continued, trying to stay with a train of thought. "I guess I have blamed him. For Lonnie. For Glenn, the guy I married. I guess I married him mostly to get out from under some memories—to get away from things—and he used to hit me sometimes, and then he left me. Then my little girl died. I found her out in the yard, and I have dreams about it still. She was almost three years old. And she was the cutest little thing." Tamma had to pause then, choking back on some dryness.

"I guess it's not a dream so much as a remembrance. One of those things you can't get rid of, so you think of it the last thing at night and the first thing in the morning, before you even know you're awake. It seems like a dream, though, because of the way I remember it. I was drinking a lot then, and things weren't too clear. I remember getting off the phone, though, and walking into the yard. I walk around to the side where the landlord had been working on the septic tank, and I start to panic. You know, how your legs go all watery and all? The ground is all soft and mushy there, and there are shovels stuck down in a pile of dirt. A concrete slab from the top of the tank sits off to the side. I'm sinking up to my ankles as I get closer to the tank, and I see greenish-gray bubbles coming up, and my heart is pounding blood up into my head. My hands are out in front of me, and I can't run because of the mud—just like in a dream when you can't run. I'm screaming now, trying to get a noise out, and I'm right over the tank. I fall toward it, and I stick my arms down into the stink of it."

Tamma was aware only of her breath when she paused, a kind of gasping and heaving. She was soaked with sweat.

"Her name was Kara," she said. There was only silence. She couldn't tell if anyone was still listening, whether someone else had been called to the phone, but she went on.

"Anyway, I just piled it all on top of him—like none of it was my fault—like it was all Coach's fault. And the doctors tried to talk me out of it, but I still don't know. I still keep thinking sometimes, what if? If this, if that. The doctors say deal with the present. Deal with what is—not should have, could have, would have. I don't know. Anyway, I saw where Coach died, and it was weighing on me like something I needed to get rid of, and I just thought I'd call. But now, just never mind. I guess he was no different from a lot of folks."

There was another pause, and the woman's frosty voice said, "Young lady, I don't know what you are talking about, but don't call back again or I'll have to get the police involved. Do you understand? Don't call again."

Tamma nodded her head up and down, staring into the mouthpiece. "I won't," she said. "I won't call again." She didn't want the police. She didn't want anything to jeopardize her visitation rights with her kids or the job Mr. Lacy had given her. Mr. Lacy had been nice about the job. He trusted her enough to let her work in his own house, take care of his own wife. She had to pull herself together.

"I won't call," she said again. "There's no reason for it."

There was more rustling of fabric, another muffled sound at the other end of the line, and right before the line clicked into its steady hum, Tamma thought she heard a woman's voice say "That bitch" or "That trash." She wasn't sure, though. She wasn't even sure she heard anything, and the confusion from that, the lack of clarity about how the conversation had ended, sent her into a panic.

She dropped the receiver into its cradle as if were a hot iron, her hands shaking. She reached for the crumpled pack of cigarettes and fished around down into the bottom of the pack with her index finger, finally hooking the last one. She smiled and laughed a throaty little laugh at her own confusion, at her fear about none of this really ending. Suddenly, though, she could hardly light her cigarette because of her trembling and sobbing. She sat slumped at the table and cried until things were just a blur and until the knocking startled her. She jumped and gave a little yelp at the sharp rap at the door. It was Louise Dodson, the Lacys' cook. When Tamma opened the door, Louise stood at the bottom step of the trailer, hands on hips.

"What's the matter with you today, girl?" Louise said. "You going to come help me with that old woman or not?"

Tamma ran her hand back through her short brown hair and took a quick, shaky puff from the cigarette. The sun was well up now, and she had to squint as her eyes adjusted from the darkness of the trailer.

"Sorry, Louise," she said. "I'm having a bad morning with a headache and all. Then I was on the phone. Sorry." She smiled down at her, an uncertain little smile, and sniffed. "I'm coming right now."

"Well, you best pull on a sweater. It's cold out here this morning, child." Louise hugged herself, pulling the front of her light coat together over her ample bosom and waist. "I'll wait right here."

Tamma brushed her hair and teeth quickly, splashed water on her face, and pulled on a bright green sweater. She looked pale against the green, but the color made her feel better. When she pulled the trailer door closed behind her, Louise said, "We best get moving. We got things to do today. Cleaning. Mrs. Lacy's physical therapist, she's coming today, too. The Missus will need help with that."

As they passed Tamma's rusted Chevette, Louise gave a little kick at its deflated tire with the toe of her white shoe and said, "And you best be getting this raggedy car fixed, too, girl. Mr. Lacy won't want no junk cars with flat tires sitting around on his land, like some of these trashy white mountain folk. You understand? I swear, some of these folks cut their grass and find cars there they didn't even know they had."

"I know," Tamma said, laughing now but still trembling slightly. She trotted along beside Louise, her hands jammed down into the front pockets of her jeans. "I know. I'm going to. I'll need to fix it by next weekend, so I can drive down to see my kids."

"That's right," Louise said. Her smile was crammed with teeth. "You'll be seeing those babies next week." The scratching rhythm of white nylon and spandex on Louise's heavy legs kept time for their march up the flagstone path to the big house.

"I get to see them the whole weekend next week," Tamma said. "Mr. Lacy's helping me with that."

"I know," Louise said. "You can think about good things like that this week. You get done the things that need doing, and then the days don't seem so bad and so long, do they?" Louise reached out with her right hand and looped it through the bend in Tamma's arm, so they could steady each other as they climbed the last steep stretch of stones that led up the sloping yard to the kitchen.

Transmigration

CECELIA'S PRESENTATION

Here's what they do. Pete and Cecelia pull into town in an old Chevy Nomad wagon, locate the YMCA, and start putting up posters. They draw a small audience—a few old ladies, some straggly looking teenagers, and maybe, if it's a slow news night, a guy with a coat and tie who will take a picture and write a little story about this for the local paper. There's no admission fee, just donations. Still, they usually take in more money this way than they do by panhandling. In fact, sometimes they take in quite a haul.

Cecelia starts. She tells them her name is Cecelia, then she introduces Pete, who is sitting next to her in a metal folding chair. They are facing a group of about twenty people scattered among rows of more folding chairs. Sometimes it's hot in these public buildings, especially in really small towns like this one, where they don't leave the air-conditioners on at night. Still, she guesses this is better than working out in the vegetable gardens back in Virginia. The vegetable gardens are what they call the fields where they grow the marijuana. Sometimes they call them the tomato fields. It's a regular cash crop operation, but it gets really hot sometimes—really hot. Today they're at a YMCA in a little place called Paulding, Ohio, and it's not too bad. They've had a cool snap here, and this is an evening meeting.

"I'm glad you joined us this evening," Cecelia says. "As you might know from reading some of our literature, we are representatives of the 'UFO Two,' who send you their greetings and want you to know that Jesus loves you and is waiting to transport you into the Higher Kingdom—waiting for you to become space travelers with Him."

Of course, this is all stuff they've made up, but she won't tell them that. She won't tell them that the "UFO Two" are really just Phil and Donna Shifflet from back in Virginia, who had this idea that some people will believe almost anything and will donate spare change at the drop of a hat. They got the idea from Jim and Tammy Bakker. If not the PTL Club, why not the UFO Club? So Cecelia explains to the good folks of Paulding, Ohio, that Phil and Donna have traveled to that next level of being, and, upon their return, committed themselves to spreading the word about the need to rise above the discordant influences of the human condition, the physical level of existence we know on this earth, in order to prepare ourselves for passing into the higher realm. The method of transportation for this passage? The same method by which Phil and Donna were transported. They were picked up by a UFO.

There are skeptics in the audience tonight. She can tell. It's hard to sell this premise in the Midwest. It's easier in the South and the West for some reason. But in the Midwest (the "buckle of the Bible belt" they like to call themselves) they'll frequently hit a real cynical group—one that thinks that every new idea is a half-baked idea. Still, folks show up out of curiosity. This looks like it could be one of those groups. The two grandmotherly types in the front row are smiling pursed little smiles at each other and are whispering something behind their hands. And there's a man in a coat and tie toward the back, who had his pen and note pad poised for notes, but now he leans forward, elbows on knees, just shaking his head back and forth slightly. It looks like she'll have to do most of the talking this evening, because Pete gets the story all balled up sometimes and just can't withstand the questions during the Q and A session at the end. Besides, the guy at the back with the pen and paper is cute, and Cecelia thinks she might be able to say something to get his attention—to arouse his interest enough so that he might want to get to know her better. At least for tonight. At least for a little while. At least long enough for them to grope and grapple with what the UFO Two call that discordant influence of lust. He has that look about him.

That's one of the benefits of all this—meeting men in different parts of the country. Cecelia doesn't always like men. But when she does like men, she likes them in the same way she likes easy credit or comfortable shoes. They do something for her. They serve a purpose, but she has a hard time thinking of them as real human beings. Men are her drug substitute, and she doesn't make any apologies.

She used to like Phil and Pete some, but they started becoming too possessive, and Donna started getting really bitchy about Phil. So now she hasn't slept with either of them for a couple of months. She thinks Pete is genuinely distraught over it, and he is getting a little weird about the whole thing. But she can't help it. If they hold her, they smother her. She has to be in control. That's what she has enjoyed about the travel—loose connections here and there—a few strapping farm boys, a local businessman or two, sometimes a sweet college kid whose head is screwed on upside down and who's looking for guidance from UFOs. Each of them unique and worth whatever risk they pose. Sometimes there are physical risks, but she feels more comfortable with those risks than she does with risks like loneliness, like failure, like the inability to hold something she might want to keep. Sometimes she feels caught in a descending gyre of failures and fear, a dark vortex from which she might be saved by orgasm. To prevent her descent, she clutches at men and things that don't belong to her, then she lets them go. That control—her ability to grab and then let go—is what keeps her floating above the darkness.

Now she watches the clean, tired-looking man in the back of the room and continues her story. His tiredness and slouch make him look at least thirty, but that's all right with her. Even though she's only twenty-one, anywhere from fifteen to fifty is all right with her. Besides, from age thirty on up, they're always so touchingly grateful, she feels like a humanitarian—like Mother Teresa.

"Reaching this next level of existence," she says, "or what some people refer to as Heaven, is really a metamorphic process, similar to the process of going from a caterpillar to a butterfly. When we pass into this higher realm, we take on different life forms, and this new life form seeks to influence the bodies of others who remain in the physical world. When we die and enter the higher level of existence, the energy we discard from our physical beings then enters the bodies of those on the lower level, thus producing such emotions as anger, hate, jealousy, and lust."

Now Pete chimes in that once we are able to overcome these discordant influences, we are free to move to the next level of existence. Cecelia wishes he wouldn't just butt in like that and say things like "discordant." Somebody might ask him what it means, and then they would have problems. She thinks Pete doesn't have a clue as to what he's talking about. Handsome, but dumb.

"Those who have thrown off the shackles of the human condition," she continues, "will be eligible to be taken up into the next level in a harvest." She explains to them that the season for such harvests is short, that such a harvest is now taking place, and that their time for travel to the next level of existence may be right around the corner. Then she explains to them their belief that members of the next level use crafts, or UFOs, to transport those on earth who are ready for the harvest. "But first," she says, "we must rid ourselves of such discordant influences as jealousy and lust and greed—focus our energies on obtaining a pure human existence."

She thinks she sounds pretty good—pretty convincing. No reason why she shouldn't. Her father, a plastic surgeon in Fairfax, Virginia, has always pushed her to excel and to not be shy about forcing herself toward the front of things. He just pushes and pushes. Lots of pushing, very little talking or touching. Her mother grew tired of it years ago and is now living with her former psychiatrist. So Cecelia learned to push, and she pushed back until it all became too strenuous. That's when she dropped out of college and started living with Phil and Donna. She doesn't feel like she's always on the verge of one of her failures there.

Usually, the money background and good schools come through and make her sound like she knows what she's talking about, even if it's all just bullshit. But now the cute guy in the back with the coat and tie is looking impatient and unhappy about being here. He is raising his hand to interrupt. This could be a long night, or this could be an interesting development.

Tom's Problem

Tom Langdon is a man with a lawn and a problem. His immediate problem is that he does not want to be at this meeting of UFO crazies. The more pervasive problem, though, is that sometimes he doesn't want a lawn, or a house, or the family that goes with the lawn and the house. Sometimes he just wants to be alone. Or sometimes he just wants to run off with a vague, nonexistent lover who will please him for a while, then leave him alone. He really has no preference. Either way, he would be rid of the lawn, and the house, and the small-town newspaper job that came with his wife. He hates the job, but he thinks he still loves his wife. Somehow, though, he thinks things would be better if he were alone for a while somewhere, anywhere but Paulding, Ohio. Sometimes, Tom worries that he is going crazy, and he wishes his father were still alive so he could ask him whether he ever felt this way. Sometimes, he thinks that if it's possible for a person to feel himself becoming a sociopath, then he is becoming one—or maybe just a hermit.

Although it doesn't occur to him, Tom has something in common with Cecelia and Pete, who sit before him spewing forth this nonsense about life forces, and next levels of being, and UFO travel. They share a confusion, a kind of fear and desire, as if they are animals milling in a pack, unsure whether to attack or mount one another. He is becoming impatient with Cecelia, though, and he wishes she would just make her pitch for money and get it over with. He wants to go, but he finds himself raising his hand anyway, and he says, "Are you saying that Jesus and Elijah and Mohammed and St. Matthew and others who reportedly ascended into Heaven in strange and miraculous ways were all space travelers—they were all aboard UFOs?"

The woman looks distressed that she has to stop her spiel right in the middle. "Yes," she says. "As to Jesus, definitely yes." She doesn't say anything about the others, however, and Tom feels compelled to ask another question, as long as there is a pause.

"This UFO philosophy," Tom says, "it sounds a little like a strange hybrid of Hinduism, Christianity, Shirley MacLaine books, and Ripley's 'Believe it or Not.' Aren't you really talking about reincarnation when you speak of purifying ourselves and getting rid of these discordant influences, this bad karma?"

"Well, not quite," Cecelia says. "Rather than the soul being recycled for purification, we are transported physically and spiritually to the next level of being, creating a kind of energy or a new life form which seeks to influence others on earth, thus giving rise to such emotions as anger, hate, jealousy, and lust."

"And the method of transportation is UFOs?" Tom says.

"Yes," she says. "That is our belief, from all of the evidence and teachings of Phil and Donna."

"The UFO Two," Tom says flatly.

"That's right," says Cecelia, and she gives Tom a look that acknowledges something between them. He thinks he recognizes the look, and he picks up just a hint of private conversation taking place between Cecelia and himself that has nothing to do with UFOs or Hinduism or the other twenty people sitting there in folding chairs.

"But this new life form—aren't you really talking about a transmigration of the soul?" Tom says. "Does Pythagorus ring a bell, or the Bhagavad Gita?"

Now Cecelia is beginning to look impatient. A kind of darkness comes over her, and she says, "No, it's not quite the same as the transmigration talked about by the ancient

Greeks or by the Hindus. But all of these people have been space travelers, according to Phil and Donna, and that's the reason for some of the similarities in their beliefs. The origins of those beliefs have just been obscured over time. But I'm sure you know that many studies have shown that UFO sightings and evidence of visitors from space exist in many of the ancient cultures, including the Greeks and the Mayans—even ancient Egypt."

"Ah, yes," Tom smirks. "The 'Chariots of the Gods' and all that. I even saw a TV program once where the guests talked about their discovery of the 'Diners of the Gods'— diggings in ancient ruins which showed that thousands of years ago space travelers built dozens of roadside diners around the world. They even had jukeboxes and soda fountains."

Now Pete speaks up. "Really?" he says. "What program was that? I missed that." It's hard to tell whether he is being serious or sarcastic, and Cecelia and Tom both stare at him for a moment before locking eyes on one another again.

"It was a joke," Tom says. "It was a comedy routine." Pete's neck and ears flush red, but he doesn't bat an eyelash. He doesn't smile. A long-haired teenager with split ends and engineer boots, sitting in one of the middle rows, turns toward Tom and says, "Hey, man. Why don't you like leave them alone and let them finish?"

"Fine," Tom says. "I don't have any more questions." He leans back in his chair and crosses his legs, ankle over knee, jamming his note pad and hands down into his jacket pockets, affecting a kind of rumpled scholar look. In fact, he does have another question. He wonders if Cecelia is wearing underwear. He can tell she isn't wearing a bra under the light jersey pullover dress, and her breasts seem disproportionately heavy and round, the way they do sometimes on thin women. Her neck looks gracefully thin with her sun-bleached brown hair pulled back, and her arms are hard and thin, as if they are used to work, her small biceps flexing as she gestures with her hands. Tom thinks she probably isn't wearing underwear.

He remembers when his wife, Anne, would do odd things like that, like not wear underwear. It was years ago. They would meet at home for lunch. Jeffrey, their oldest, was just a baby then. The big old clapboard fixer-upper on William Street, which they eventually bought, was stifling in the Ohio summer heat, and Anne would be at the stove stirring something that sizzled in the frying pan. She would be naked except for an apron, open at the back, and Tom would come to her and press against her, kissing the back of her moist neck, reaching around beneath the apron. Her sweat was like syrup. After making love and eating lunch, Tom would go back to the newspaper, where Anne's father was the publisher and editor, wondering if the old man could smell his daughter on him—wondering if her father hated him because of that or if it was something else.

Now, Tom doesn't go home for lunch, and Anne doesn't wait for him at the stove. Now she jogs during her lunch hour. Tom doesn't jog, and he can't understand how people get pleasure out of it. He bets Cecelia, the UFO lady, doesn't jog. And he bets she isn't wearing underwear and that she doesn't care one whit whether the lawn gets mowed. He stares, unfocused, toward Cecelia and Pete as the two drone on. They are starting to make their pitch about the Life Force Institute in Virginia, how they are busy trying to spread the word throughout the world, preparing people for the harvest to come. They talk about how much money such an undertaking costs, and how every little donation helps.

Tom can't believe that any of these people will donate

money. Then he remembers his own checkbook, and he remembers he forgot to check the balance when he took it from the dresser that morning. He slips it from the inside pocket of his jacket and peels back the navy blue cover slowly, as if trying to sneak up on the balance column. The balance, in Anne's flowing felt-tipped handwriting, reads $17.59. "Shit," he says under his breath. He replaces the checkbook and jams his hands back down into his jacket pockets.

Never quite enough, he thinks. Always something. The dental bills alone for Ben's enamel problem are eating them up. Jeffrey has always been healthy, and Tom knows that's a blessing. They had no money and no insurance when he was born. Anne got pregnant their last semester of college, so Anne's father paid for the wedding and, a few months later, the birth of his first grandchild. He gave Tom a job at the newspaper and, since then, he has given him precious little else. The old man does give Anne some spending money once in a while, but it goes. It just goes. It all disappears for things like the house, like the bills for the little caps on Ben's baby jaw teeth, which are disintegrating from a congenital defect that causes chronic vitamin deficiency. It's an ailment that makes Ben tiny and pale. He is only a toddler, but he already has the teeth of an old man.

Anne deals with it all with such maddening calm, while Tom worries. In the face of money problems, a sick child, the lung-compressing dullness of small-town life, Anne is able to sleep like a clear-eyed child, deeply and long, her head nested in her feather pillow as if it were her grandmother's bosom. Tom sleeps in small fits, just on the edges of dreams, so he remembers his dreams when he wakes up, adding to the subliminal baggage he carries with him during the day. Lately he has been having nightmares involving cloaks and blackness. When light enters the room at dawn, illuminating Anne's long, dark hair and her smooth brow, revealing a peace that must mean deep trust, he wonders how he could ever think of leaving, why he would ever think of other women.

So when daylight comes, Tom worries. He worries about money and Anne and about what is wrong between them. He worries about the boys, especially Ben, and what will become of such a delicate child. He worries about himself and why he feels like a hermit and why he can't sleep. And he daydreams. While out shopping with Anne at the mall in Fort Wayne, while holding little sticky boy hands tight to keep them from disappearing among the huge indoor ferns and waterfalls, he daydreams about the beautiful woman in the short leather skirt about ten yards ahead of them, and how he could catch up with her and walk beside her, and they could quicken their pace so Anne and the boys couldn't keep up, and they could just keep going until Tom felt like being alone again. Alone, sometimes, feels natural to him.

Alone is how he feels now in this room full of people at the YMCA. He focuses again on Cecelia, though, and realizes that she has been staring at him. He gives her a slight, acknowledging smile, then he daydreams about her long, thin arms and legs, her delicate neck.

PETE'S SOLUTION

Pete has decided. He's decided that if the guy in the back of the room, the one with the smirk and his fancy-ass questions about Hindus and Greeks or geeks or whatever, makes a move on Cecelia tonight, he'll put a stop to it. He'll knock some fucking sense into him. Coat and tie, Elijah and bad karma. Piss! Guys like that from a little place like this don't have a clue what they're getting into with her. He has put up with this shit long enough. Then he thinks he has to get hold of himself. He's tipping toward the edge, getting full of those discordant influences again, just like Donna says. She says just because Phil and her still sleep together, Pete shouldn't be jealous. She says the same thing when Cecelia and Phil sleep together, even though it's her own husband. We need to purify ourselves and get rid of those feelings. She says that's why she and Pete should sleep together, too. To purify themselves by getting rid of those lust feelings. That's why Phil says he watches them sometimes, too. So he can purge his feelings of jealousy. Sometimes Pete feels sorry for Donna and Phil—that they can be so stupid to think he's that stupid. But he plays along. He doesn't mind bopping Donna. He wouldn't kick her out of bed for eating crackers.

He can hardly help himself though when it comes to Cecelia. Lust and jealousy. She makes him crazy, and he thinks he loves her, although he's not exactly sure what that means. He knew this was going to happen if they made this trip together—that she was going to drive him nuts.

Cecelia says Phil and Donna are just users—that they are all just users—and she calls the harvest a lot of bullshit. Pete agrees with her mostly, but sometimes he looks back on it and he thinks Phil and Donna have really helped him in a way. He's found a place where he almost fits in. And he thinks they have something here about getting a grip on these goddamn discordant influences. Sometimes he's so full of them he wants to do damage to somebody.

Sometimes he tells people that he was really messed up for sure before he met Phil and Donna. He had no folks to speak of—just the old lady in Lynchburg. And he ran off from there when he was fifteen. Once, when he lay with his head against Donna's breast, she asked him about his mother, and Pete said, "Folks always runnin' off from her—my sister before me, the old man before I was even out of diapers. She's a claw, a real bitch. And she doesn't give a flying shit about anything except her beer and cigarettes and her overtime pay from that spooky, raggedy old shoe factory." Donna stroked the back of his neck and hair after that.

Before he met Phil and Donna, Pete and Bill Haynes were doing an insurance scam down in Tidewater—muscling little old ladies to buy life insurance that they didn't need and that wasn't worth the paper it was written on. Pete felt bad about that sometimes. But the time he had to beat the lady up because she wouldn't pay her monthly premiums anymore, that made him feel really bad for a while. Then the police were hot after him, and that's when he ran to the mountains and hooked up with Phil and Donna at the farm out in Dyke. They picked him up hitchhiking along I-64. They got him interested in this religion scam of theirs, and pretty soon he started sleeping sometimes with Donna. He plays along as if he is really sincere about what he and Cecelia call "this UFO shit," and he's decided that it's a little bit spooky that Phil and Donna would think that he would think they know what in the hell they're talking about. But he plays along. He likes Donna and Phil and some of their UFO clan OK.

Then he met Cecelia and that was it. That's when he started feeling like he had a sense of direction—toward her. He's never felt this way about anybody. Never this jealous. He'd do just about anything for her. And he would never use her the way she uses folks—the way she steals from people. Oh, he's done plenty. He would never deny that. He has stolen money and hurt people with his fists and feet. But he's never stolen the self of somebody—the way Cecelia does. What she does is worse than stealing somebody's property. She drains dry the souls of men, takes away something from each of them, like a hunter with no regard for the season and no regard for the delicacy of the prey. There's no joy in her sport. He's seen her wreck families and not even blink. She's in town for three days somewhere, and lives that have been settled for twenty years have to settle themselves again in some new and hurtful way, maybe on some new part of the earth. She hobbles folks in a way that slings and crutches can't fix. So Pete has no reasonable explanation for why he thinks about her so much, why he feels like he needs to do something for her. Sometimes he thinks of hurting her. Fists and feet—as if that's all they both need.

It's different guys all the time now on these trips, and it's making Pete crazy. He knew they shouldn't have made this one together. He just wants her all to himself all the time. He's thought lately that he might as well put a stop to it. Might as well start. Some changes are due. She'll see that he means business, and maybe she'll see what's important. He can't let it get out of control, though. He almost whispers it to himself—that he has to watch out for those discordant influences. But for now, he has to sit here in front of all these hicks and listen to Cecelia try to cop some money for the trip, a little pocket change to keep them going to Denver, where they're supposed to pick up the package at the airport. Phil and Donna said it's a really important shipment, very risky, and that's why it has to come in at Denver. Good stuff. Street value that would knock your eyes out. He smiles to himself about Phil and Donna and this UFO shit and what some folks are willing to believe about other people. Sometimes it's almost as if Phil and Donna can't see it—like they almost really believe in themselves. It's really hard to figure what goes through the heads of some folks.

Night Flying

After the UFO meeting, Tom Langdon lingers for a while on the front steps of the YMCA scribbling a few notes into his pad. He has to write something about this, after all. Mostly, though, he is waiting to see if she approaches him. He thinks he was getting signals from her, but he's not sure. His thoughts about what might happen are vague. The dangers must be considered. She's young, perhaps mentally unstable. This is a small town. Who knows where she's been or what she's done—and with whom? Somehow, all of these things clashing together in his mind excite him even more. The possibilities are endless if he just lets his imagination go.

He waits just long enough so that it doesn't appear as if he is really waiting for anyone, then turns to leave. He is a few steps down the sidewalk when he hears her voice from behind.

"Excuse me," she says.

"Yes?" He turns toward her, very businesslike, his tone impatient.

She walks straight up to him, her hands clasped together in front of her, her fingers laced, her upper arms hugging her breasts, pushing them forward. Tom has to concentrate to watch her face rather than the thin jersey front of her dress.

"I noticed you were taking notes," she says. "Do you work for a newspaper or something?"

"Yes. The *Paulding News-Press*." His smile is almost apologetic.

When she smiles back at him, Tom can see that she has the kind of straight teeth that come from braces, a brightness and alignment that money rather than nature gave her. He also notices, up close, the tiny, feathery lines that are starting to spread from the corners of her eyes and mouth, as if her surface is beginning to crack. Maybe too many years of lying in the sun, or hard living, or both. It's hard to see under the streetlights, but her skin seems to have a kind of yellow quality, as if a tan she might have had several weeks ago has faded with illness or reclusiveness.

"I hope you won't be too hard on us," she says, still smiling. "You didn't look very pleased with our presentation."

"Pleased?" He has to restrain himself, to keep himself from blurting out what he really thinks, just in case he is wrong about her—just in case she is truly committed to such foolishness. "No. I'm curious, though. Why do you do it?"

"Do what?"

"Why do you go around doing this thing—whatever it is you do?"

"You mean teaching about the harvest and space travel?"

"Yeah."

"Well, maybe we could talk about it," she says. "Can I buy you a cup of coffee somewhere around here?"

A total stranger has asked Tom out for a cup of coffee. Yet, somehow, he understands it to mean: will you sleep with me? So much for the power of words, he thinks. For all the good language does, for all the power contained in a well-chosen phrase—all of that is lost when the essence of all that is intended with whatever words that are spoken is: will you have sex with me? A thought flashes—that maybe, indeed, that is the power of language.

"Sure," says Tom. "I'd like a cup of coffee." Then he thinks of being seen, of having to explain things to people he might run into. He quickly tries to think through how this might be arranged. "But I have a couple of stops to make before I'll be free. Can I meet you somewhere later?"

At the top of the concrete stairs, Pete steps back into the shadows to listen. Part of his job has been to replace all the metal folding chairs in their carts along the wall of the auditorium. The kid with the gritty, heavy-metal hair and the engineer boots has helped him, asking questions the whole time, wanting to know all about the space travel part of the harvest. Pete answered as patiently as he could until, finally, he had to tell the kid to get lost. Now the little old ladies from the audience, who had been dawdling and chatting in the hallway, pass Pete at the doorway as they leave. They smile pinched little smiles at him and nod good evening. The heavy-metal kid is still lurking around inside the building somewhere. Pete remains quiet and hidden in the shadows for a moment.

Down on the sidewalk, Tom casts his thoughts ahead quickly, already picturing himself helping Cecelia to lift the jersey dress over her head, sliding it over her long, thin arms, dropping it to the floor.

"Where are you staying?" he says. "Maybe I can meet you there later."

"Clover Leaf Motel, down the road in Van Wert."

Perfect, Tom thinks. Van Wert is about ten miles south of Paulding, along the highway headed toward Columbus, and is just enough bigger than Paulding that he is less likely to run into someone he knows there.

"Perfect," he says, "because the restaurants here will be closed by the time I'm free. There's a place in Van Wert that's open all night, though."

"Perfect," she agrees, smiling her money-bought grin. "It's room 18 at the Clover Leaf."

"About ten-thirty OK?"

"Sure. Fine."

Suddenly Tom remembers Pete, her partner.

"What about your partner? Will he want to come for coffee, do you think?"

"Do you want him to?" she says, giving him that stare again, that look that speaks many languages at once.

"I just wondered."

"I'm pretty sure Pete has some things to do this evening. I think I can tell you what you want to know about us."

"OK, then," Tom says, loosening his face slightly into a tiny smile. "About ten-thirty."

"Fine."

Pete, standing back in the shadows, has overheard these arrangements and is hurriedly trying to think through some plans of his own. Just then the kid with the heavy-metal hair, who said his name was Rob, comes slouching out of the YMCA, his mouth hanging open slightly, looking dazed and at a loss as to what he will do next. Pete clasps him around the shoulder suddenly and guides him down the steps toward Tom and Cecelia. Pete smiles into Rob's face and talks to Cecelia at the same time.

"I was just talking to my new friend Rob here, and he wants to know more about the UFO Two. Don't you, Rob?" He squeezes Rob's shoulder in a friendly fashion.

"Sure," Rob says, shaking shaggy hair back out of his face, flipping it over his shoulder.

"How about your new friend, Cecelia?" Pete says, gesturing toward Tom. "What's his name?"

"I'm sorry," Cecelia says, turning toward Tom awkwardly, her palms turned up in question, "I didn't catch your name."

"Tom Langdon," he says, eyeing all three of them coolly. As soon as he says it, he wishes he had given them some other name.

"Well, what about it, Tom?" Pete says. "Do you want to

know a little more about our little group?" Pete watches Tom and Cecelia trade looks.

Cecelia says that she and Tom might continue their little discussion later. She seems to glare at Pete, but Pete ignores her tone and the glint of hardness in her eyes.

"Fine," Pete says. "That's fine. You two go on, and Rob here and I will meet you later. How about that?"

Tom is confused by the arrangements. He doesn't have his car, he says. He explains to Pete that he has some errands to run, that he will need to go home to get his car, and he will meet them in Van Wert. Tom is beginning to lose his courage and enthusiasm, however, and is undecided whether he will go to Van Wert.

"Let us give you a lift to your car then," Pete says, clapping Tom on the back. "We can drop you and Cecelia off."

"No! No, that's OK. I can walk. I do it all the time."

"Oh come on, Tom," Pete says, putting an arm around Tom's shoulder now, nudging him toward the Nomad parked at the curb. "We don't mind giving you a lift. Do we, Cecelia?"

"He said he wants to walk."

"It's no trouble," Pete says. "No trouble at all."

Tom's thoughts scatter amid speculation about which course will be more dangerous—to refuse or to comply. It's a fool's choice, he decides. And he has already been a fool to let things go this far. Without really making a choice, without much more intent than to at least see out a course that has begun, he lets himself be guided to the passenger's seat of the Nomad. Four doors slam around him, locking him into a hazy, passive decision. He leans heavily in the seat, as if he will sink through to the floor, overcome with a sadness and fear at the thought of what might be lost now.

Goose flesh begins to raise the pale hairs on Cecelia's

arms. She thinks Pete is switching into his aggressive, physical mode and is acting just a little hyped. He does strange things sometimes when he gets that way. He frightens her sometimes. Although he has never hurt her, he can be physically intimidating and absolutely irrational when he gets all worked up.

When he was going through his fits of jealousy over her and Phil, he would lapse into little dramas, pretending to be high on something when she knew he wasn't, thrashing around a room uncontrollably, just like a child in a tantrum. If they had sex after one of these little fits, he would cry and cling to her. As she sits in the back seat of the Nomad now, next to this strange teenager with the Frankenstein boots, she watches the backs of both Pete and Tom, and she sees how it would be between the two. Pete is powerful and is talking a mile a minute about how much he likes this farmland. Tom is slight and is scrunched into the corner of the front seat, staring out the window at the clean clapboard houses that they pass, nodding and issuing one-word responses as Pete rambles on. What, she wonders, are they all doing here?

What am I doing here? Tom wonders. His stomach is lurching. His thighs burn with nervousness. They are traveling up William Street, the route Tom has given Pete, and will be in front of Tom's house in just a matter of seconds. He will think of something—some way to bow out—when they stop to drop him off.

"This is it coming up on the left," Tom says.

Ancient knotted oak trees guard the front lawn. As they approach the house, Pete swings from the right lane into the left and glides along the curbing that edges the front sidewalk. Every window shade is open and it looks as if every light in the house is on, as if there might be a grand party going on inside. The long windows of the old house throw wedges of yellow out across the shaggy lawn.

Tom sees one of the boys moving around in the front bedroom upstairs. He's not sure who it is because he can only see the top of his head, and both boys have identical crew cuts now. Then he sees Anne running through the dining room from the kitchen. For an instant he wonders why she is running, until he sees the top of another little crew cut bobbing along behind her just above the level of the window casement. She and Ben are playing a chasing game of some sort, and he can see now that Anne is laughing. Everything seems magnified in the light of the house. Anne is wearing jean shorts and a white T-shirt, and Tom thinks he can see her biceps flex as she picks up the child. Ben is squealing and giggling as Anne hoists him into the air above her head. Tom and the others in the car sit motionless and silent, eyes toward the golden windows, as if movement might break the spell within the house.

Then Tom sees his wife lifting their child through the air, soaring with him from room to room, running through the living room, under the archway and back into the dining room. The child is laughing and breathless, his sticklike arms and legs outstretched as if he were a superhero winging his way through the house, borne aloft in his mother's arms. She has given the power of flight to a weak, sickly boy.

In that instant, Tom wants to be there with her, inside the source of light rather than outside looking in, and he starts to open the car door. Pete has left the motor running, though, and just as Tom starts to put his foot out, just as he is turning to thank him for the ride, Pete jams the car into gear, and the car leaps forward. The door slams closed with the movement, almost catching Tom's foot. The tires spin in the loose chat along the curbing, and Pete swings the car quickly into the other lane, heading north on William Street.

"What are you doing?" Tom says, leaning away from the door in case it should fly open. "I need to get out."

"Now what, Pete?" Cecelia says from the back seat.

"Just shut up for a second," Pete says. Both hands are on the steering wheel, and he looks as if he is concentrating hard on keeping the car on the road. The car picks up speed quickly as they move up William Street. They are already on the edge of town where the houses become sparse. Soon there will be nothing but fields and fields of corn and beans, and William Street will become Highway 127, which shoots straight north to US 24. There they will have to choose—east to Defiance or west to Fort Wayne, Indiana. In either case, they are not headed toward Van Wert.

"Look," Tom says, "I've got to get back. You'll have to let me off." He is almost yelling to overcome the roar of the wind whipping in a cross-current through the open windows of the Nomad. He glances back quickly and nervously at Cecelia and Rob in the back seat. They are both shaking their heads, brushing at their eyes and mouths with their fingers, trying to keep their hair from wrapping around their faces in the wind. Cecelia's hair has fallen loose and some is stuck to her lips.

Cecelia spits at the hair and yells at Pete, "Damn it, what are you doing? You're going the wrong way!"

"We're all taking a little trip," Pete yells back. "This is the next leg of our journey—so to speak." Tom can see in the green glow of the dashboard lights that the driver is smiling to himself slightly. "Fort Wayne and then keep going west. We have an appointment to keep."

Cecelia leans forward over the back of the bench seat and slaps Pete on the shoulder, not hard, but more like the way a sister would slap a brother. "These guys are not going with us, Pete."

"Not all the way. But for now they are. Right guys?" Pete glances to his right and back over his shoulder, his hands still gripping the wheel at ten o'clock and two o'clock.

"Sure, man," Rob says from the back seat. "I'm along for the ride."

"You've got to let me out," Tom repeats firmly.

Pete leans forward, still gripping the steering wheel with his left hand, and reaches under the edge of the front seat with his right. He pulls out something with a metallic glint in the dim light, something with mass, something that carries weight, and rests it against the inside of his thigh on the seat. He drives with one hand now. Tom and Cecelia both see the movement, just as was intended, and Tom draws back into the corner of the seat. Cecelia says, "Pete? Pete?"

The driver looks straight ahead and says, "Don't sweat it, man. Just a little incentive for you to come along for a while. I'd hate to have to whack one of your knees." Even as he says it, Pete doesn't really know what he will do. He's not sure what he hopes to accomplish except, perhaps, some truth. Maybe if everyone in the car takes a good, hard look at what they're doing, then he will have accomplished something. Beyond that, he has no plan.

They ride in silence for a moment, the Nomad sailing through the flat fields of northern Ohio on its way to Fort Wayne, until Pete says, "Hey, Tom, you wanted to know more about the UFO Two and the harvest, right?" No one says anything in response, so Pete yells into the wind, "Well, isn't that what you wanted with Cecelia back there?"

"Pete, stop this now!" Cecelia yells back.

Pete turns his head and shoulders toward Cecelia, his nostrils flaring, and shouts, "Stop yelling at me, whore!" In the instant that he turns, the wheels of the Nomad drop off the edge of the highway and onto the chat-lined berm. Gravel and dust kick into the air as Pete jerks the car back onto the paved portion of the road at sixty miles per hour. The tires scream as he straightens it out to regain control. Tom has braced himself with one arm, his hand flat against the dashboard. The color has drained from his face. Cecelia is pulling herself up, leaning forward over the back of the seat again.

"You're going to kill us, you dumb shit!"

Pete starts to laugh then, and says, "No I'm not. I'm gonna save us. I'm saving us from not making choices. After tonight, folks are gonna have questions that need real answers. No more bullshit. You go in a direction, and you take what comes with it. And if you think some hurting doesn't have to come along with it, then you're dreaming in fucking la-la land." No one says anything for a long time, until Pete says, "Now, Sister Cecelia, why don't you start telling us some more about the harvest while we ride."

She slumps back into the seat, as if pouting.

Pete says, "Hey, Cecelia!"

She stays quiet for a moment, but then she begins, her voice quivering and thin. "It's a metamorphic process—passing from one level of human existence to another level of existence."

The wind still roars through the open windows of the speeding car, so that Cecelia's voice is barely audible. Her words are indistinct, sometimes sounding like nothing more than a hum, a kind of "aum" sound. Still, the others try to listen, turning their heads this way and that to avoid the roar and whistling in their ears. They know the story already, and none of them really believes it. But without it, this would just be a short, frightening ride to Fort Wayne, where they must decide what risks they are willing to take. On either side of them, flat bean fields stretch to the dim, dark horizon. It's as if they are sailing along a taut trimming, a narrow bridge between two great oceans that lie still and dark in the haze of a moonless night. As Cecelia drones on into the sound of the wind, the Nomad's headlights reach forth and snatch at the next stretch of blackness into which they are about to fly.

Gathering Bittersweet

HERE'S WHAT I thought of in the waiting room—that it's like having a snake or a spider inside me, waiting to strike, waiting to take me down into blackness. It's repulsive and yet it's a part of me. It's something deep inside that has been there for a long time now. I've lied to myself for a number of months, and I've lied to my wife, Anna, with my silence. My appetite's been less and less. I'm tired, and the icepick stabs in my side are getting worse. Now I can feel it, as if I can just reach right in and actually touch it. Something hidden beneath the roll of beer fat around my waist has taken shape. It has a life of its own. It's a part of my liver, Dr. Kinney says. I'm a butcher, so I can just picture it—a growth the size of a grapefruit, hiding there in the darkness like a thief in the night.

Now I look out at these people from behind the chipped enamel meat case. I've known them for years, some of them all my life, but I don't understand what they're talking about. They smile and laugh. They talk to me. They want something. What is it? A pound of ground beef—lean. Six butterfly pork chops. Tony, is the ham I ordered ready yet?

Their voices run together in a kind of gibberish that reminds me of the talking the old folks used to do in Grandpa Novac's cleaning shop on King Hill Avenue, where they would argue and laugh and cry about the old country. That's what it's like this afternoon. Everyone is from the Ukraine or Poland, and they're speaking in the old languages, bearing old grudges and starting old wars. It all clashes. They're speaking English, of course, but I can't follow what they're saying. I only pick up vague hints here and there.

It's a gray afternoon, and Goosey's Market is even darker than usual. It was beginning to spit snow when I walked back to the store after lunch. I had an appointment with Dr. Kinney at lunchtime, and Anna was there in the waiting room when I arrived. There are times when you see something or someone and the sighting is harmless—even pleasant maybe. But when you see the same thing under certain circumstances, you feel nauseated. You feel as if your knees will hyperextend.

Anna and I have been married thirty-three years and have lived here in St. Joseph all our lives, but she's never come to a doctor's appointment with me. Old Doc Kinney delivered our two sons. He's set our broken bones, given us shots for infections, and stitched our wounds. He gave my wife pills to help her sleep after our youngest son ran his motorcycle into the side of a truck and was killed. But in all those years, we've never been in the doctor's office at the same time. Anna smiled and waved when I saw her in the waiting room. I smiled and said, "Hi, Hon. What are you doing here?" I knew why she was there, though, and I felt my knees weaken. There was a burning sensation at the back of my thighs and up into my buttocks as I fought back an urge to empty my bowels. That's when I thought of the snake or spider inside of me. But I smiled.

That's when the doctor told us how bad it was. The thief should arrive in the night within three to six months. That's why Anna was there today and why we cried in each other's arms. Doc Kinney held our hands and he cried, too. When we left the doctor's office, I thanked him. I don't know why—I just always seem to thank people.

Now I'm thanking Mrs. Kawalski. "Thank you, Mrs. Kawalski. You be careful with those groceries now. I hear it's getting slippery out there. Do you want Ronnie to help you?"

I'm beginning to have some clearheaded moments now that the gray afternoon has become a biting, snowy evening. There's something depressingly uncertain about overcast afternoons. But the weight of such days seems to lift as the contrast sharpens, as the lights from the store reflect off the large front windows that separate us from the blowing, black night.

Goosey didn't want me to come back to work this afternoon. He said I should take some time off. I told him I had to work to keep my mind on something. Now the work is over, and Goosey is in the back room doing the day's paperwork, and I go back to say good night.

"Jeez, Tony, take a couple days off, will you? You and Anna spend some time. Okay?"

"Maybe I will. I don't know. Maybe I'll take my vacation. I've never taken vacation in the winter." I tell Goosey I'll think about it and I say good night again.

I've been the butcher at Goosey's Market for a lot of years. I know every inch of the store, from the freezer in the back to the curb out in front. The wooden floorboards of the store are wavy in places and have been worn shiny over the years. We never shine them, though, just spread sawdust and sweep. Sometimes the stock on the shelves is a little unorganized, but our customers know where to find things. We still have a stock boy, Ronnie, who sweeps the front sidewalk every morning and evening. I get a good feeling when I see that clean sidewalk in the morning. My step seems to have more bounce on a cleanly swept sidewalk. During hot, dusty spells, the push broom leaves short, neat combed streaks in the light gray dust. Then the sidewalk smells like new life when a late afternoon thundershower throws down huge drops that evaporate on contact, then become steam. If it keeps coming, the rain washes the remaining dust into the gutter and down the street past the post office.

As I walk to the front display window, I see the snow is coming very heavy now. I can barely make out the Merchant's and Farmer's Bank across the street. The flakes start as pinpoints up by the streetlight and enlarge as they twirl toward my face. They seem to disappear before they hit the glass. Maybe the walk home in the snow will clear my head.

The way is white, no footprints. The streetlights cast blue shadows behind trees and into the corners of the yards that I pass. Golden light falls from windows onto sparkling lawns. People and houses and streetlights that have been my friends for so long line the way, but the snow makes an old trip seem new. It might seem odd to some folks to feel safe in a snowstorm. I've always felt comfortable in the snow. I'm not nervous driving in the snow, even when it's very deep, and I almost never get stuck or stopped, even on a freshly powdered hill. "Everything is under control," I like to tell Anna when she gets nervous about my driving in the snow. "Everything is under control," I would tell the boys when they were small and the lights would go out in a storm. "Everything is under control." But the numbness in my snow-crusted feet seems to have spread to my head. Things aren't any clearer. Too many things rush back and come together and clash with other things.

My chest heaves in sweet stabs of cold air as I mount the

front steps of what has been our home for almost twenty-five years. Our sons were just little boys when we got this house. Now my throat constricts, my eyes and my nostrils are hot. I'm fumbling, and I can't understand how to get the front door open. I look at different parts of the door—the hinge, the windowpane, the lock, the knob. None of the individual pieces tell me how the whole door can be opened. I give quick glances to the left and right, up and down the porch. My nose is running and is dripping off my lip. Finally, I turn the knob and push the door open. I step stiffly into the front hall, see that I'm dripping snow from my shoes and cuffs, then I step back over the threshold and pound my feet on the porch. I just pound and pound, stamp and stamp until Anna comes from the kitchen wiping her hands with a blue-flowered paper towel.

"What in the world are you doing?" she says. "Just kick your shoes off at the door and come in. Don't stand there stamping all night."

"I don't know what I'm doing," I say and look up at her. Mucus and spit and tears are running down my face. The snow on my eyebrows and hair begins to melt and mix with the other moisture. I need a towel. Anna hands me the paper towel she's been using. I press it to my face and squeeze my nose, my eyes. The towel smells of her hands and her kitchen and begins to crumble as I blow hot moisture in and out in heavy puffs.

"We need to call Michael," I say, "to tell him what the doctor said."

"I called him this afternoon," she says. "We talked about it, and I told him it didn't look good. He said he was going to come right down this evening."

"Well, I hope you told him not to! It's too bad out. Besides, he can't just take off from work because of this."

"I told him that's what you'd say—that there's nothing he can do right now."

"Shoot," I say. "He's just going to get stuck somewhere. He shouldn't try to make it from Iowa on a night like this."

"I know, I know. I told him what you'd say." She seems to forget her next thought. "But I'm glad he's coming. It'll be good that he's here. I don't know." Anna's voice cracks and trails off as she slumps down into the stuffed winged chair that sits just inside the living room archway. She curls her feet up under her legs and lets her head sag to one side. She stares at the coffee table, her shoulders pinched forward. "I just don't know what to do," she says dreamily. "Michael will know." She just stares.

"There's nothing to do," I say. "It'll be good to see him, though. But darn those roads."

"Michael will know," Anna sighs.

She doesn't understand what it is to be a son and a man. Michael is just a boy in the same way that I'm still a boy. It's the same way old Goosey is still a boy sometimes. Things get confusing, things don't work out. A man gets worried and doesn't know exactly what he's going to do. A little boy is afraid and wants to cry and wants to run and hold tight to the big pant leg that's so sturdy and comfortable. The boy is a man, though. The boy is me and it's Michael and it's even old Goosey sometimes. That's not hard to understand. Michael won't know what to do—any more than I do. Nobody should expect him to. When you come right down to it, nobody knows, really. I'll tell him everything is under control.

"Anna," I say. "There's no point in doing anything. What do you expect to do?"

Again, she stops to think—to weigh out what is left.

"I want to grow old with you," she says and turns toward

me. Her lower lip is vibrating. "We're supposed to grow old and have grandchildren who come and visit. We're supposed to have weddings and births and Christmases and Thanksgivings."

"Christmas dreams, Anna," I say. "Those are just Christmas dreams. Remember when you were a kid? You would have dreams, visions of what Christmas would be. But it was never quite as good as the anticipation."

"We had wonderful Christmases!" Anna says, irritated. "We gave the boys nice Christmases, all holidays, wonderful."

"I know. That's not what I'm saying. The point is, you have a few here and there that stand out, that seem the way they're supposed to be, and then others are just flat. Things don't always turn out like you hoped."

"Oh, really?" she says, and glares at me, as if I'd done something hateful toward her. "You think you need to tell me that?" She looks away and sits stiffly.

I pad into the kitchen and sit down at the table, too exhausted to try to think through what I'm trying to say. I bend to rub heat and blood back into my feet, but the stab in my side straightens me with a jolt. My neck is pounding, and small spots of glitter dance in front of my eyes. I rub my socked feet back and forth on the warm linoleum and lean back to rest. Anna has fixed sausage with milk gravy, hominy, and bread. The gravy is for the bread. It's one of my favorites. I already know what will happen though. I'll prepare my plate—salt and pepper everything just to my taste. I'll savor the steam. I'll take one or two bites, then stop and stare at the food. I get angry just thinking about it. I want to taste the sopping bread and gravy, feel the crunch of the fried sausage, the pop and burst of the fatty pockets of salty grease. But after one or two bites, I'll be full. That's something about this whole thing that makes me mad. Early satiety I think is what Doc Kinney called it.

Anna is moving around in the kitchen now. She talks more about Michael coming, as if his visit should be the center of our thoughts and discussion. "I hope he didn't have trouble getting someone to teach his classes," she says. "I think he's a little worried about his contract for next year."

"I doubt that," I say. "But I do wish he wasn't trying to drive down tonight. The snow and his job. It's just too much." Then I think, to hell with it. He can come and see us at a time like this.

It's so hard to figure how kids will turn out. Maybe you have some expectations. Nothing specific. Just vague notions of how your kids will be as adults. Who knows what happens along the way? Michael has always been the hardest to read. Even though he's careful about a lot of things, he seems to accumulate and discard some things carelessly, neglecting them in subtle ways until they disappear. He has lived with women rather than marrying them. They're thinking about making him an associate professor in Iowa City, but he's told us that he doesn't like it, that he might leave, that he has no passion for teaching English. He seems bored with everything, including his mother and me, and he has an irritating way of quoting from this book or that poem, as if they contained all things necessary to get a person through life. What a smartass he is. I miss him and want to hold him in my arms again, as if he were a little boy.

With Jack, our youngest, it was different. You could read his needs and his feelings in his open face and open arms. He wanted to be loved for everything that Michael wasn't. His too loud laughter was meant to endear. His carelessness was an invitation to hug him. He made us smile, laugh, then he died. Sometimes when I'm missing Jack, I just stare into space.

"I'm sorry, Anna," I say. "I can't eat this." I push my plate away. I've made only a few dents in the mound of bread and gravy.

"I wish you would try a few more bites," she says. "You need your strength. This not eating is probably why you're so tired."

"The reason I'm so tired is what Doc Kinney said today. The tumor is damaging the liver. He says I'm going to feel tired, start losing my memory, things like that."

"I know, but . . ."

"But what? But what? What in the hell do I need energy for anyway? You don't need energy to die. It's just the opposite. Think about a battery!" Ill temper. Irascibility. That was another thing the doctor said to watch for.

She won't look at me and stares at the tabletop. She doesn't blink even though droplets have welled up at her lower lids. "We need to talk more about treatments," she says.

"I already said I don't see the point in doing anything. I'm not going to waste my time and our money shopping around for miracle cures. I'm not going to spend my time in a hospital. My home is here, you're here. I just want to go to the store in the mornings, play poker on Friday nights, go to Mass on Sundays. Nothing fancy in the way of sin or redemption, if you please, but to hell with hospitals and treatments."

My voice has become whispery thin and shaky, like it does when I talk seriously in front of other people. Anna lowers her eyes and gently rocks her head from side to side, just staring, tensing the muscles in her jaw and throat to choke back tears. She will lapse into such trances of grief over me now, just as she still does over Jack.

"Anna, look," I say. "Look at what we've had. We've had a life together. We've had some times that we could freeze and call happiness. Some folks never have that."

"I just want more."

"Then have faith that there will be more. It just won't be more of the same."

Silence settles over the dishes, and I rise slowly and squeeze Anna's shoulder as I walk to the TV room.

I sink back in my recliner and switch on the television with the remote control. The evening's paper is folded in a dog-eared, careless manner next to the chair. Anna has been sitting in my chair this afternoon, probably trying to nap. She hasn't slept well at night since Jack died. I watch her pass back and forth in the kitchen doorway. She hasn't put on much weight over the years, but dark crescent moons hang under her eyes, and her mouth is creased. Parallel tendons of skin droop from her chin to her collarbone. I try to remember her as a young woman, when we were first married, but I can't. And suddenly, that failure overwhelms me with more sadness than anything else about this day. I have to conjure up other images, an event or a place, and try to place her there.

I can picture a fall day. My father's car. We couldn't afford a car of our own yet, but sometimes we would go for drives in the country in my father's 1947 Chevrolet. We would drive up and down the gravel roads in the rolling hills south of town. A fine film of gravel dust covered the dashboard. The high banks and wide ditches, layered with tall, drooping foxtail grass and short sumac trees, were coated with the same white film. The powder shook from the leaves of grass that were sucked into our breezy wake. It must have been October, and it was still warm. Indian summer. The sky was high and clear, and Anna's cheeks were flushed with the warmth of the afternoon. Her shoulder-length hair, curled under gently at the ends, whipped around in the breeze and would fly back off of her neck, a neck so delicate it seemed too thin to hold her head straight. Sometimes a piece of hair would wrap around her face and into her mouth, and she would crinkle her nose and flip the hair back with a hand motion and the tip of her little finger.

We were going up a steep grade between two high, sunny banks when Anna said, "Stop, look! Look at that!"

I slammed the brakes and slid to a stop in the gravel.

"What? I don't see anything. Where?"

"Up there." She pointed and craned her neck and shoulders out of the window. "It's bittersweet. Let's pick some, and I can make a pretty centerpiece for the table."

I could barely see the hard, tiny, dark orange berries high up on the bank. Anna was already out of the car and scrambling up the bank while I pulled the car off the road. I climbed the bank behind her and picked through the dusty leaves looking for the scruffy, vinelike branches and orange berries. We gathered several handfuls of the branches, then crossed to the other side of the road to a lower, less steep bank. We sat there for a while against a sagging pasture fence and kissed. Then we stepped over the fence and down into the hay pasture that sloped down from the crest of the bank. We lay on the grass and made love there, on the side of the hill, in the sunshine. I was surprised—even a little embarrassed. But as we lay in the prickly stubble of mowed hay, staring up into infinite blue, I thought then that we were indestructible—that what she and I contained within us and what we held for each other was as limitless and cloudless as that expansive sky. That might have been the day Michael was conceived, and it was one of those times you want to freeze.

Then we both heard the faint whirring and churning for the first time and sat up quickly, Anna clutching her blouse to her breasts. On the side of the next hill, beyond a small grove of cottonwood trees, maybe a hundred yards away, was a farmer bouncing along on his tractor, throwing up disked earth and dust behind him. He saw us looking in his direction and he waved, a broad, whole-arm movement that you would use if you wanted to get someone's attention. I waved back with an arched motion from the wrist and smiled, as if I were acknowledging a friend. Anna and I looked at each other, burst into laughter, and fumbled for our clothing. We laughed and leaned on each other all the way back to the car and to town. Laughing. Leaning. We've had a few of those times. Some folks haven't had that.

And that thought—the thought of the absence of such things from so many lives—plunges through my chest now, pushes me down into the chair with such a weight that I want to make a noise from my throat, but I can't. I try to raise my hand to wave at someone across the room—a young woman smiling at me, raising her own hand in greeting. "Hi, Hon," she says. I try to say something back, to bring something out of my mouth, but it won't come. I try to raise my hand again, but it's paralyzed. Then I see that the young woman is Anna, and she's waving to me in the waiting room at the doctor's office. Something tightens around me, webs of darkness and shortness of breath. I realize that I've been crying again, just at the edge of a dream or memory, where there are no bright lines between joy and grief and fear.

I pitch forward with a rush of dread, and a pain knifes through me. My arm is numb where I've been leaning on it, sunken back in my recliner. The telephone is ringing and it startles me, drilling into my bowels. Scattered images jump around. The snow. Michael. The telephone. Jack. Anna is answering the telephone.

"Michael?" she says. "Where are you, sweetheart? Are you all right?"

My limbs relax, and I sink back into the chair for a few seconds before rising slowly to go stand by Anna in the dark hallway. She is motioning to me. Michael wants to talk to me.

"He's still in Iowa," she whispers as she hands me the phone.

"Hi, Michael," I say. "What's the matter, son?"

"Hi, Dad. I'm stuck in Leon, Iowa."

"What happened? Snow bog you down?"

"No, the snow's not really that bad here. It's something to do with the fuel injection system. I'm at a service station just off of I-35. The problem is, the mechanic here says he might not be able to get the part I need in Leon. He might have to send to Des Moines for one, and it could take a few days."

"Well, listen," I say. "I'll come up there tonight to pick you up and then drive you back when it's finished."

"I don't know, Dad. Mom says you really got a lot of snow there."

"I think it's let up some," I say. "If it's too bad, I'll just turn around and call you."

"Well, OK—if you think you can make it," he says. There is a pause before he continues. "But listen. One of the reasons I want to come down is because Mom said you were thinking about not taking any sort of treatments for this thing. But I want you to think about something, and then we can talk about it. Are you there?"

"Yes, I'm here. What is it?"

"There's a guy I know in Iowa City. He's an oncologist. Really sharp. Anyway, I called him this afternoon after Mom called. He said they're doing some exciting things with liver cancer treatments at Johns Hopkins and at Sloan-Kettering. They're experimental things, you understand, but I just wanted you to think about it."

"What's exciting about these treatments?" I say. "Are they like going to a Royals game or an amusement park or something?"

"Jeez, Dad. You know what I mean. They're actually doing something, you know. Slowing down the tumors, giving people more time."

"Oh, you mean experiments to prolong things—make it drag out a little longer."

"You don't have to make it sound like Dachau. I'm just trying to help. They probably have people standing in line waiting to get into these programs."

"Like Dachau."

"Damn it, Dad!"

"That's enough!"

"Is life really so awful, Dad?"

There is a slight hum on the line. Anna stands nearby, pulling a sweater tight around her.

"No, it's not," I say. "But it can be sometimes. It can be damn awful. I guess this is all just part of it."

"I'm sorry, Dad. It's just that I'm scrambling, trying to figure out what to do. I don't know what else to do."

"I know the feeling, Michael. I know it well. Just give me directions to where you are."

Anna pours me a Thermos of coffee as I put on my boots and heavy parka. I can't find my good leather gloves, but I find a pair of brown cotton work gloves in the pocket of an old coat hanging on a hook by the back door.

Hushed powder covers the shadowed neighborhood as I tramp out to the garage to warm up the Impala. Only a few sparkles are falling now, and it looks like they're falling from the trees rather than from the sky. I stop at the garage door and listen, but I don't hear any distant sounds—only my own breathing and the muffled squeak of the snow under my boots. While the Impala is warming, I go in to tell Anna not to wait up for us. It might be early morning by the time we get in.

"Oh, I'll probably fall asleep in the chair watching TV," she says. "*Hill Street* is on tonight."

"That's right. I forgot."

"Be careful, and turn around if it's too bad."

As I back out of the driveway and fishtail slightly down through the powder, I see that a car hasn't made the turn at the end of our street. It's gone over the small embankment in Mrs. McLaughlin's front yard. The front of the car is stuck nose-down in her lilac bushes. It looks like it's the Czuprinski kid's car from down the street. I guess he couldn't get it out, so he just left it. Probably scared old Mrs. McLaughlin half to death.

I get out to look at the damage. The stiff lawn under the snow has been peeled and scraped into hard chunks where the frame hung up going over the bank. Two of the lilac bushes are damaged, probably snapped off at the base. The branches are wedged under the front of the car. Michael and I can help Eddie Czuprinski pull the car out tomorrow. We'll clean up these bushes, and then, this spring, I'll get out here and repair the lawn. I'll have to cut those lilacs back and prune the others. In a couple of years there will be some uniformity to them again.

I pull the door to the Impala open and lose my footing for just a second. I catch myself by twisting sideways and hanging on to the door handle. There is an explosion of fire in my stomach as I stretch to remain upright. The streetlight above the intersection spins, then goes upside down as I topple backward into the front seat of the car, letting my head snap back and bounce off the seat. My feet hang over the edge and rest on the metal strip that says "Body by Fisher." I lie still for a moment to let the pain subside and to decide what to do about picking up Michael. I just rest and breathe.

The pain starts to fade to a low burning sensation, and I pull myself up by the steering wheel. My hands are steady now, and the cotton work gloves wrap comfortably around the tan plastic. Now that I'm sitting up and my hands are on the wheel, I've decided. I'll go get Michael, and tomorrow we can pull this car out of here. We can talk to each other more easily when we work on something together. I take a deep breath and put the Impala into gear. Just a little pain now. The car doesn't handle badly along this little stretch of road. I don't understand why people have so much trouble driving in the snow. You just have to get a run at the hills and throw it out of gear and pump the brakes when going down. Take it easy but keep going, that's all.

I turn slowly from our street onto Lake Avenue, where only a few tracks mark the way that others have gone this evening. The old neighborhood is beautiful with its fresh wrapping, so cold and clean. Everything is in sharp focus now that the snow has stopped, now that the moisture has been frozen right out of the air. A neatly furrowed path has already been plowed down the center of King Hill Avenue, and as I head out toward the highway, the night sky beyond the headlights seems to glint like dark enamel, or like a mirror that you could just reach right out and touch. I wish Michael could be here beside me right now to see this. Then maybe he could see that we don't need to do anything. This car handles fine. Everything is under control. If it's like this all the way, I'll see my son in no time.

Gaytha Lindensmith

ABOUT THE AUTHOR

A native of St. Joseph, Missouri, MARK LINDENSMITH is a lawyer who has been writing fiction since 1986. He has been awarded several residency fellowships in fiction writing at the Virginia Center for the Creative Arts, Sweet Briar, Virginia. His stories have appeared in publications such as *New Letters*, *South Dakota Review*, and *Wind* magazine, and he has had legal articles published in numerous magazines and books. He and his wife, Gaytha, live in a rambling old farmhouse in Earlysville, Virginia, with their six children, four of whom are quadruplets. He is working on a novel, for which he recently received an individual artist grant from the Virginia Commission for the Arts.